A note from the edito

Well, this is it—the last
We've had a good run,
things have to end son
Temptation is very, ver

When we celebrated our twentieth anniversary last year,
we personified the series as a twenty-year-old woman.
She was young, legal (well, almost) and old enough to
get into trouble. Well, now that she's twenty-one and
officially legal, she's leaving home. And she's going to
be missed.

I'd like to take this opportunity to thank the countless
number of authors who have given me, and other
Harlequin Temptation editors past and present, so
many hours of enjoyable reading. They made working
at Harlequin an absolute pleasure.

I'd also like to thank our loyal readers for all their support
over the past twenty-one years. Never forget—you are
the reason we all do what we do. (Check out the back
autograph section if you don't believe me.)

But this doesn't have to be the end....

Next month Harlequin Blaze increases to six books,
and will be bringing the best of Harlequin Temptation
along with it. Look for more books in THE WRONG BED,
24 HOURS and THE MIGHTY QUINNS miniseries.
And don't miss Blazing new stories by your favorite
Temptation authors. Drop in at tryblaze.com for details.

It's going to be a lot of fun. I hope you can join us.

Brenda Chin
Associate Senior Editor
Temptation/Blaze

"You're trying to distract me," Tess said, her voice a little more breathy than she would have liked

"Who? Me?" Evan said innocently. "Tess, if I were trying to distract you, I'd do something like this." He barely moved his fingers and flicked open the clasp on her bra.

And just like that, Tess was half naked in Evan's bed.

It occurred to her that at this precise moment she might not actually be the one in charge.

"Evan McKenna, you will get your clothes off right now, reach your hand into that sack and grab a condom of any shape or flavor and get inside me within the next ten seconds, or I will spend the rest of my life making you regret it." There, she'd told him.

He ripped off his shirt. "All you had to do was ask."

"After that crack, you'd better be the best I've ever had."

He ripped off his jeans and grinned wickedly. "Don't worry. I will be."

HEATHER
MacALLISTER
NÊVER SAY NÊVER

HARLEQUIN®

TORONTO • NEW YORK • LONDON
AMSTERDAM • PARIS • SYDNEY • HAMBURG
STOCKHOLM • ATHENS • TOKYO • MILAN • MADRID
PRAGUE • WARSAW • BUDAPEST • AUCKLAND

ISBN 0-373-69225-0

NEVER SAY NEVER

Copyright © 2005 by Heather W. MacAllister.

This edition published by arrangement with Harlequin Books S.A.

® and TM are trademarks of the publisher. Trademarks indicated with ® are registered in the United States Patent and Trademark Office, the Canadian Trade Marks Office and in other countries.

www.eHarlequin.com

Printed in U.S.A.

Dear Reader,

I'm particularly excited about *Never Say Never* because all four Harlequin Temptation novels this month are stories about friends who find that life takes them in different directions.

In *Never Say Never,* my heroine, Tess, gets a really big tip—a duffel bag full of money and a hunky man named Evan to help her spend it. Every woman's fantasy, right? Find out how Tess and Evan spend the money, as well as what happens to her friends this month in *Good Night, Gracie* by Kristin Gabriel, *The Eleventh Hour* by Wendy Etherington and *Her Last Temptation* by Leslie Kelly.

Part of the fun of writing the connecting stories was getting to work with the other authors—and justifying time spent in a bar as research! The not-so-fun part was knowing that these four books would be the last Harlequin Temptation books published in North America and the four of us, like our heroines, would be going in different directions.

Exactly ten years ago this month, my first Harlequin Temptation novel, *Jilt Trip,* was published. What I've enjoyed about writing for Temptation was that I was encouraged to develop my writing voice and was never reined in—well, hardly ever. Creatively, it doesn't get much better for a writer.

I want to thank those of you who've written and e-mailed me to tell me that my books have made you laugh or forget your troubles. I appreciate it and hope you'll read our goodbye-to-Temptation books and let us know what you think. You can find out more about me and my upcoming books by visiting my Web site at www.HeatherMacAllister.com.

Best wishes,

Heather MacAllister

To my editor of ten years and fifteen Temptation novels,
Brenda Chin.

It's been a great run and, thanks to you, I will never write a
book without explaining the protagonist's goals up front,
tightening the first three chapters, or hearing your voice
tell me to add sexual tension. Eh?

Prologue

"HENRY, I'M THINKING a couple of those shiny little fish would make me a fine set of earrings." Tess Applegate set a snifter of 100-year-old blended cognac on the scarred oak table. Her customer, whose hat dangled with a dozen fishing lures, grinned in delight.

"Let me know which ones and they're yours." He reached for the cognac.

"I've got my eye on that long teal-green one over your left ear, but I haven't decided for sure yet. Besides, it might be the very one that would catch you a big fish."

"Lord, I hope not," Henry muttered as he held the glass at chest level. "It's not about the fish, Tess. It's about the journey."

Whatever. Tess watched Henry go through his ritual with the cognac. It was always the same. First, he held it to the light, admiring the color even though there wasn't much light in the bar. Then he held the glass close to his chest. That's the point he was at right now.

Usually Henry was dressed in a business suit that looked expensive, even though it was always rumpled. Tess suspected the elderly man had been told to lay off the booze and drove all the way to Temptation, a bar in small-town Kendall, Texas, to sneak a snort after work.

Now Henry brought the snifter closer and gave a little sniff. Tess guessed that was why it was called a snifter. Then he practically put his nose in the glass and inhaled. Honestly, the first time he did that, Tess thought he was trying to drown himself.

She was glad she'd talked Cat and Laine, the owners of the bar, to invest in the cognac. Henry really enjoyed the stuff and always left her a nice tip.

Of course, if things didn't go their way with the Historical Preservation Society in court this afternoon, Henry and his hefty tips would be no more.

Tess wiped the already clean table in the booth next to Henry as she looked out the window for Cat. It was impossible not to notice the big old machines already parked and waiting to widen the road, courtesy of the city or the county or whoever it was. Never mind the businesses like Temptation that lined the road. Just tear them down. Rip out the trees. Pour concrete. Obliterate history.

"Today's the day, Tess?" Henry didn't miss much.

"Yeah. Cat and Laine are at the courthouse now. We could be closed by the time you get back from your fishing trip."

"It'll all work out." Henry had a Yoda Zen thing going for him. Everything he said sounded profoundly wise, even though sometimes it didn't make much sense.

"I hope so," she said without looking at him. This place had been her home, and these women her family, for the past couple of years.

Henry swirled the amber liquid. "If the bar has to close, look on it as an opportunity."

"Yeah, an opportunity for unemployment." Though she didn't want to admit it, bouncing around the country and changing jobs every few weeks had lost its allure. That's why she'd stuck around here for so long.

"You can follow your dream."

"I don't have a dream, unless it's to make it through closing without my feet hurting."

"Sure you do." Henry cupped the tulip-shaped glass and inhaled again. "If Temptation closes, it'll give you a chance to launch that singing career of yours."

In spite of her worry, a smile tugged at the corner of her mouth. Bless his heart, he was serious. "That's right, I could. All I need is time, talent and money."

"If you've got the first two, it shouldn't be hard to get the third." He took a tiny sip of the cognac and held it in his mouth.

Tess had tried that once and her tongue had gone numb. She just didn't get how something that cost six-hundred bucks a bottle, wholesale, burned her tongue the same as a six dollar bottle of tequila. She'd rather have a beer.

Well, maybe not. Something had happened to her metabolism when she'd hit thirty. She'd thought her jeans had shrunk. They'd been known to, but only in the waist? Not likely. So she'd cut back on the beer. It wasn't that she'd ever drunk that much, but that depended on who defined *much*. And lo and behold, her jeans fit again. Yeah, things had a way of working out like that.

But now, she could use a beer. Laine and Cat had figured they'd be back by late afternoon. Maybe the fact that it was taking longer than expected was good news.

"Will you sing for me before I go, Tess?"

"I'm not really warmed up, Henry," she said.

He nodded.

A car door slammed, footsteps crunched over the gravel, and then the front door opened and slammed so hard it bounced back open. One look at Cat's face told Tess what she wanted to know, as if the slamming hadn't.

Cat headed straight for the bar, Laine right behind her, and Gracie, the bookstore owner from next door, stepped inside and quietly closed the door behind them.

Gracie slipped onto a bar stool near Laine, and Cat went behind the bar. She grabbed a cocktail shaker, filled it with ice, and started shaking it. Hard. Tess figured now wasn't the time to point out that she hadn't put any liquor in it.

"It's over," Cat announced.

Tess left her bar towel on the table and headed for the three women. Though she'd been expecting the news, she felt, well, sucker punched. She figured Gracie and the Sheehan sisters felt worse. Gracie's bookstore occupied the other half of the building and the bar had been in the Sheehan family for twenty-one years. The sisters had taken it over from their mom, Brenda, just before Tess had arrived on the scene.

She hitched herself onto a bar stool next to Laine, who clutched a piece of paper.

"I knew those stuffy biddies at the Historical Preservation Society would reject us." Cat tried to pour a drink and when nothing came out, she yanked the top off the shaker and added vodka and the rest of the fixings for a Cosmopolitan, their signature drink. It had started as a joke because Kendall was as uncosmopolitan as a place could get, but they did a fair business with the drink.

Yeah, forget beer. A Cosmo would hit the spot.

Laine pushed her glasses up her nose and stared at the letter. Over her shoulder, Tess could see phrases like, "Thank you for applying" and "Unfortunately doesn't qualify for registry in our society."

Cat set the drinks in front of them. "The city wants a new road, so we're out. Did you really think we'd change anything tonight?" she asked her sister.

"Where am I going to store all those books if I can't find a new place by the end of the month?" Gracie asked.

Where am I going, period? Tess wondered. "I'll never find another job as good as this one." She wished she'd kept quiet. Compared to what the others had lost, it sounded trivial.

Except it wasn't to Tess. She'd settled here after a decade of rootless wandering. She'd liked being alone and free to go wherever she wanted until she'd met the Sheehans and Gracie. She was still free to leave, but she wanted to decide when it was time, not have it forced on her.

"How are we going to explain this to Mom?" Laine asked.

Tess reached over and patted her hand awkwardly. She wasn't the touchy-feely sort, but Laine was. "Brenda will understand. She'll be pissed, but she'll deal with it."

"I just can't believe it." Laine fought back angry tears.

Tess sipped her drink. Okay, she gulped half of it. Crying people made her nervous.

"Had faith in the system, Lainey dear?" Cat taunted her sister.

"Yes, I did." Laine crumpled the letter. "This isn't right. How can they just take away everything we've worked for?"

"Because they can." Gracie took a sip of her drink.

Drinking was a good idea, except Tess's was all gone. She eyed the shaker longingly. As the others talked, she poured the dregs into her glass.

They were already making plans. Tess didn't do plans. When she was younger, living the wandering life had seemed fun, fresh and spontaneous. She avoided responsibility and she avoided the work stress that plagued so many of the customers who came into the bar after work. Just the thought of being in an office building again gave her the heebie-jeebies.

But now…now what?

There was no place else she wanted to work in the

tiny town, but she'd suck it up and apply at the diner if the others planned to stick around.

"Who are you kidding?" Cat muttered.

Tess glanced at her. "Did you say something?"

Cat smiled and shook her head. "Just making plans." She met Tess's eyes and Tess knew Cat was telling her she needed to make plans, too.

Feeling jittery, Tess stood. In the mirror behind the bar, she noticed the empty booth. She'd forgotten all about Henry and he'd left without saying goodbye.

That wasn't like him. Wondering if she'd ever see him again, Tess retrieved the bar towel and went to clear the booth. She couldn't help noticing that her usual twenty-dollar tip wasn't there, but she hadn't earned it today.

Tess wasn't big on money as long as she had enough to cover her modest needs, but with the construction on the road starting, business had been down and so had her tips. She'd run short last month and hadn't paid all her rent. And it was already a week into the new month.

She hated worrying about money, so she wasn't going to. Something would come up. Something always did.

Henry's glass wasn't there. How weird. Tess stared, then noticed a lump in the booth seat. It was a navy duffel bag. Henry must have left his fishing stuff. Tess looked out the window in case Henry's old car was still parked out front, but it wasn't there. She didn't have a cell number for him. In fact, other than his fondness for expensive cognac, she didn't know much about him at all.

She checked for an ID tag on the duffel so she could call his home and leave a message, but there wasn't one. Instead, there was an envelope with her name on it.

It was heavy cream paper and the sheet inside was monogrammed.

Dear Tess,
This is a beginning, not an ending. You've got the time and you've got the talent. I'm backing you. Go to Nashville. Record. Make your dream come true.
                                    Henry Bartholomew
P.S. I want a copy of the CD.
P.P.S. I took the glass and the bottle.

Nashville? CD? Was he insane? Tess hauled the bag onto the table and unzipped it.

It was filled with money. Lots and lots of money.

1

"IF UNCLE HENRY HAD WANTED you to know where he was going, he would have told you."

The smugness in his cousin's voice made Evan McKenna grit his teeth. Doing so caused a pang in a molar, or maybe a couple of molars, but he didn't want to think about it. He didn't have time to think about it.

Neither did he have time to drive all over rural Texas chasing down their Uncle Henry, but that's what he was doing.

He unclenched his jaw, closed his eyes and drew a deep breath—now what was he supposed to visualize? Oh, right. Pristine white beaches and waves ebbing in—or was that flowing?—and slapping the shore and the feel of warm sand between his toes... except he didn't like sand between his toes and there was always trash beneath the surface of beaches because where was he supposed to find pristine beaches anymore, anyway? Not in Texas. And how boring was it to just lie around on a beach when he could be...

Evan drew another breath, annoyed that this relaxation technique only caused him more stress. In fact, relaxing caused him stress. Relaxing was overrated.

Impulsively, he reached through the privacy window dividing the driver from the passenger and flicked the chauffeur's cap off his cousin's head. Evan immediately felt better. Action worked every time.

"Hey." Woody repositioned his cap.

They sat in one of the company limousines on the side of the road next to a garage in some little town, Woody driving, Evan passengering.

"This is where you left him?" Evan asked.

"Yeah."

"What was he driving this time?"

"An old red Ford."

"They're all old." Their uncle had old cars stashed in several places around the state. "I don't suppose you know the license plate?"

"No," Woody said. "He made me leave. I only know he's driving the red car because it's not here now."

Great. Just hunky-dory. "So you don't know where he is?"

"Nope. And I wouldn't tell you if I did."

Evan sized up his cousin, wondering if he could take him. Woody was what? Nineteen? Looked like he'd been working out. Hmm. Maybe not. "When did you get to be so self-righteous?"

"I dunno. Maybe it's the uniform or this really tight hat." Woody checked his reflection in the rearview mirror. "Or maybe it's the car." He reverently ran his hands over the padded leather steering wheel of the limo. "The ladies love this luxoboat."

Evan smiled to himself, remembering his summer of chauffeur duty. "If you knew anything, I could get it out of you."

"Not this year."

"I might have to pay you more, but you do have a price." Evan was willing to pay it.

He could see Woody's face in the rearview mirror and saw the wince, but no weakening.

"To my surprise, I find that something—some-one—is more important than money."

Evan groaned. "Is that integrity I hear?"

"I know. Surprised the heck out of me, too. But you're looking pretty ragged man. I'm with Uncle Henry. You *need* this vacation."

What Evan *needed* was to find Henry and get him to rescind the stupid order that was keeping Evan out of the Bartholomew's Best corporate headquarters. He knew his uncle meant well, but sometimes he wasn't practical. Make that most times. "I am not on vacation. It was a forced lockout."

"Just go with it. It won't be forever."

"In the retail business, three weeks *is* forever. Twenty-one entire days in which I am not allowed to contact anyone, access my computer or set foot in the building. I can't even get one tiny daily report." Evan leaned forward. "How much would you charge to write tiny, daily reports, Woody?"

"If you got a daily report, it wouldn't be much of a vacation."

"This is *not* a vacation! You prepare for vacations. I had no time to prepare."

"You were warned."

"I didn't think Henry'd actually go through with it," Evan muttered. "The entire management team is on vacation. And if they're not there and I'm not there, then no one is running the store. Literally. Henry must have forgotten he gave everyone vacation at the same time."

Woody snorted. "Sure he did."

"He needs to be reminded of the possible consequences." Like missed ordering deadlines, liability issues, new product announcements, theft, inventory, and the fact that family-owned, cash-rich Bartholomew's Best department store was constantly fending off takeovers. Somebody had to watch Henry's back, and that somebody was Evan. He owed him. Now, if only Henry didn't make repayment so difficult. "Woody, you know I should have been left in charge."

Woody shrugged. "I'm just the chauffeur."

Evan tried another tack. "He's getting older—"

"Oh, you would be so busted if he heard you say that."

"I think I've already been busted, Woody."

"Not to add to your already overflowing brain, but could you please make an effort to call me Quatro?"

His cousin, burdened with a lengthy family moniker and attached numeral, had been looking for a new nickname. Evan massaged the back of his neck muscles with both hands. "You sound like a gang leader."

"I sound cool. Quatro is working for me. *Toy Story*

ruined Woody. I mean, being Woody was great in middle school, but not so good in high school."

"Woody is a cool name. Think Woody Guthrie."

"Who?"

Evan exhaled. "Woody Allen."

"Auugh!"

"Woody Harrelson?"

His cousin shook his head.

"Woody of Jake and Elwood."

"Who?"

"The Blues Brothers. Ultimate cool."

"Before I was born."

Evan felt old. "Okay—Woody Woodpecker."

Woody met his eyes in the rearview. "You meant that in the cartoon sense and not in the slang sense that every other human on the planet means it, didn't you?"

"Uh, yeah."

"I rest my case."

Evan supposed he'd better humor his cousin or he'd never get any cooperation.

"Hey, what's up?"

"Nothing," Evan said before realizing that Woo— Quatro's—cell phone had buzzed and he was talking to someone else. Evan hated it when people did that.

He dropped his head back onto the seat. He wanted a drink. Maybe even alcoholic. And why not? He wasn't driving and he didn't have to stay sharp for any meetings. Uncle Henry did stock an excellent bar. Evan unlatched the burled wood cabinet in the panel in front of him.

It was empty. Evan blinked. There had been a bottle of something dark and smoky in there for as long as he could remember. Something that manly men who ate red meat and smoked cigars and made deals on golf courses drank. Power in a bottle.

Thoughtfully, Evan closed the cabinet. "Hey." He nudged his cousin.

"Gotta go. Later." He straightened and placed both hands on the wheel. "Where to, sir?"

Evan ignored the attitude. "So…*Quatro*, have you ever driven Henry to any bars around here?"

Woo—Quatro beamed at the sound of his nickname. "Sure. Lots. And diners and cafés and truck stops."

Evan nodded to himself. He remembered the drill from his own chauffeuring summer. "Any around here?"

"Yeah."

Maybe Henry was still there. Evan gestured. "Head on out."

Quatro hesitated.

"What?"

"I'm trying to decide whether to mention that Uncle Henry had a navy blue duffel with him, as well as that camo one he likes."

"You should definitely mention it." Evan's breath hissed between his teeth. "So he's playing fairy god-father again. This makes it easier. Roll down the windows and listen for screams of joy."

As Quatro rolled down the tinted window, Evan rolled his eyes. "I was *kidding*."

The window went back up and Quatro drove the limo onto the road.

"You aren't going to try to talk me out of looking for Uncle Henry?" Evan asked his cousin.

"No."

"Why not?"

"You're supposed to do things like go on a pub crawl when you're on vacation."

"I'm not on vacation," Evan reminded him, but without heat.

"I wish he'd force *me* to take a vacation," came from the front seat.

Evan was making a real effort to think of Woody as Quatro, but it wasn't happening. "I chauffeured Henry the summer I was nineteen. Trust me, this is a vacation with pay."

"No, lifeguarding at the club was a vacation with pay." His cousin gave an exaggerated sigh. "Did you do that?"

"No. Golf caddy."

Quatro shuddered. "Not my game, golf. And here we are. Wayside Diner and Good Eats."

The place looked fashionably retro, but Evan could see that it was never-changed retro. Just the kind of place that would appeal to Henry. He got out of the car, walked inside, ordered a bottle of water and was given a paper cup with ice, water, a plastic lid, and a straw. When he tried to pay, he was waved away.

"Does a man named Henry come in here?" Evan sucked down half the water.

"Sure. I packed him a bag lunch a few hours ago. He's going fishing." The woman at the counter gave him a friendly smile. "You know Henry?"

"My great-uncle." Evan responded to the curiosity in the woman's face.

Henry mandated that those who worked at Bartholomew's Best mingle with people as a way of keeping in touch with the buying public, and Evan didn't mingle much. This was a prime mingling opportunity.

"You favor him."

That couldn't be good. Henry had forty-five years on him. "I don't suppose he mentioned if he was going to a fishing hole anywhere around here, did he?"

"No." The woman's eyes narrowed. "He didn't tell you where he was going?"

"He never does. He just takes off. I wanted to catch him before he got good and started on his trip, since there's no way I can find him after he disappears." He dredged up a smile to reassure the woman.

She wasn't all that reassured. "Sounds like you want to bother him."

"Absolutely."

"And he doesn't want to be bothered."

"Nope."

The woman laughed, but didn't seem overly excited, so Evan guessed Henry hadn't left her any navy blue duffels. "Are those brownies?" He pointed to dark brown squares on a plate behind the glass counter.

"Made fresh today," the woman replied.

"How about wrapping me up a couple? My cousin is out in the car and I don't think he's eaten for at least forty-five minutes."

"Teenager?"

"Yeah." Evan wandered to the cash register as the woman bagged the brownies. "Eating all you want—those were the days."

"Oh, I hear you." She rang up the brownies.

Evan passed her a five-dollar bill and waved off the change the way she'd waved off his money earlier. "If Henry passes this way again tell him…" Tell him what?

"That you're lookin' for him?"

"He probably already knows. Just ask him to check in. Not that he will." Evan smiled to show there were no hard feelings.

There. He'd made actual conversation of a non-work nature with a human other than a relative. Henry would be proud.

When he got back to the car, Evan broke off a chunk of brownie and handed the bag to Wo—Quatro. "Don't eat and drive."

Quatro snapped his phone shut. "I thought that was don't drink and drive."

"That, either." Evan climbed into the back seat and stuffed the whole chunk of brownie into his mouth all at once. Good. Very good. Had he eaten lunch?

Closing his eyes, Evan leaned his head against the padded leather and savored the chocolate taste. He didn't know he liked brownies this much. He didn't know he liked food this much. Maybe it was because he usually did something else while he ate and didn't pay attention to his food. Technically, he was riding in a car now, so that counted as doing something else, but he could also be working on his laptop and that would have been a threefer. Excellent use of time.

But his laptop was locked in his office.

Man, this brownie was good. He'd have Quatro swing by the diner on the way back to Austin. He'd buy more brownies. A dozen. And he'd eat them for breakfast.

"Wake up, dude."

The car had stopped. Evan blinked. "I fell asleep?"

"You took a power nap."

"I don't nap." Evan finished off his water. "What time is it? How long—"

"I let you sleep about fifteen minutes." Quatro peered at him through the privacy window. "I hate that hit-in-the-head feeling you get when you fall asleep at the beginning of class and don't wake up until everybody leaves. That's too long. You feel like trash."

"You fall asleep in class?"

"Just Myth and Mythology. Man, I learned all that stuff watching *Hercules* reruns. Besides, any name sounds Greek if you add *cles* to it. Quatrocles. Sounds good. Evancles." There was silence. "Maybe not."

Evan declined to comment. "So where are we?"

"We're at this bar Henry likes."

Evan looked out the window. The word Temptation scrolled across a sign. The building was all apples and vines and faux Tudor. "This is a chick bar."

Quatro went still. "You mean, like…lesbos?"

Evan yanked his attention back to his cousin's hopeful face.

"I mean it looks a little too decorated for a neighborhood honky-tonk. Women have clearly been involved."

"Oh."

Evan opened the car door.

"Hey, I'm supposed to be doing that." Quatro belatedly exited the car.

"We can skip the door formalities."

"I'm thirsty anyway," Quatro said casually. "So I thought I'd go inside with you."

Evan figured there was no way his cousin was going to stay in the car. "Soft drink, water, juice."

Quatro gave him a disgusted look. "I'm driving. I'm not an idiot."

"You're underage."

"That, too."

Evan considered telling Quatro that he could ditch the hat and uniform jacket, but decided not to. Dealing with people's reaction to him was all part of being a chauffeur.

What Evan hadn't counted on was people's reaction to him being accompanied by a chauffeur.

He pushed open the door, swept his gaze over the dark interior, taking in the stained glass lamps and a really interesting mural featuring Adam and a lushly endowed Eve, before becoming aware that conversation had literally stopped.

The place was nearly deserted, but a cluster of women huddled by the bar was watching him. Right in the middle, propped against a couple of bar stools, was a navy blue duffel bag.

"I see Henry has been here," he murmured.

But since there was absolute silence, everyone heard him.

A tall woman wearing a short skirt propped her hand on her hip and her spike-heeled boot on the bar rail. "Damn. I knew there was a catch."

HE WAS A SIX-FOOT-TWO, good-looking catch, Tess admitted to herself.

Well, easy come, easy go. She hadn't wanted the money anyway. She'd just remove enough to pay for the glass and the bottle of cognac Henry had taken and give the whole shebang back to this... Tess eyed him more closely. Oh, no. He was one of those. She recognized that hollow-eyed look he wore—she'd seen it on her father often enough. The guy was exhausted. Another drone working himself to death.

Not that he'd admit it. He might not even know it. His type rarely did. Tess knew his type. Once upon a time, she *was* his type. But not now, and not ever again.

However... Their gazes collided and his eyebrows twitched upward. Hmm. A little interest there. Maybe he wasn't that far gone. He might be worth salvaging.

Or maybe he wasn't one of those. Maybe it was just that the kid next to him had zapped all his energy. The kid had bright eyes and a scruffy goatee that all the boys his age seemed to grow these days. "Is this a..." He gestured toward the bar and practically danced from side to side. "I mean, it's okay that we're in here, right?"

"Woody." The exhausted man closed his eyes.

Tess followed the kid's gaze. Cat, Laine and Gracie all leaned toward each other. Cat had her arm around Laine. There might have been some cleavage visible from the kid's angle.

Oh, for pity's sake.

Tess turned back to the man-child, approached him, and assumed her best buddy-you-aren't-any-where-near-man-enough-for-me stance.

Then she looked him up and down, lingering on his teenage, hormone-laden package. Lingering long enough for him to move his hands protectively forward. A corner of her mouth curled upward. "I guess you can be in here." She included them both in her smile before walking her extra-tip walk back to the bar. "Take a seat."

She turned and looked over her shoulder to find them with identical mesmerized expressions. Yeah, the walk got 'em every time and the drone looked as if he were on a company expense account. Always good tippers. "Be right with you."

Leaving the duffel at the bar, she snatched two napkins and coasters, and walked back to the booth—the very same booth Henry had recently vacated. "What can I get you two to drink?"

They were still staring at her. Maybe she'd put a little too much into the walk. Maybe she should stand up a little straighter and tone down the sexy, world-weary waitress act. That usually played better after five o'clock and a few beers, anyway.

"I'll have whatever is on tap," the overworked one said.

"I'll have—"

"Coke or Sprite?"

"Man. I don't even get carded?"

Tess gazed down at the kid. The male ego was such a hopeful thing and yet so easily crushed. And just as easily glued back together.

"Your age has got nothing to do with it." She tapped the bill of the chauffeur's cap he'd set on the edge of the table. "You're the designated driver. And I have to admit, I have a thing for designated drivers. I find it an incredibly *sexy* thing to do." She paused, giving him a direct look and holding it until she saw she had his complete attention. "They come in with their friends and drink sodas or juice while everyone else cuts loose. Then they make sure the group gets home safely." She gave a little sigh. "Very manly." She smiled. "Sprite or Coke?"

The kid straightened and his shoulders broadened, manly pride restored. "Coke."

Tess glanced at the kid's companion and caught his knowing gaze. She lingered a split second, long enough to register his warm approval, and then stalked off, forgetting to put the extra sway in her hips and annoyed that she'd liked the fact that he approved of what she'd done.

She didn't need anyone's approval, especially a precociously burned-out rich boy.

Yeah, she'd seen the limo through the wavy bottle glass windows. At least he didn't make his driver wait in the car.

She drew the beer herself, as well as the Coke, and carried them over to the booth.

The drone gave her a bland smile. "If you're not too busy, would you get yourself something to drink and join us?"

Tess had been hit on before, but never so politely. Make that emotionlessly. Or maybe carefully. That was it.

She hooked a thumb over her shoulder. "This is about that bag, isn't it?"

He shifted his eyes toward it. "Not exactly."

"Yeah, right. But don't worry. I'm not a thief." Tess went to get the duffel. It wasn't as though she wanted the cash. That kind of money came with a lot of responsibility. It was just that she would have had a heck of a good time getting rid of it.

She'd barely had time to absorb the possibilities of all that dough and when the possibilities started creeping into her thoughts, accompanied by flickers of excitement, she'd known she had to get rid of it.

Chasing wealth wore people out even after they caught it. No amount was ever enough. As soon as they had it, they found stuff to spend it on. And then they wanted more of it to spend on more stuff. And then they abandoned everyone important in their lives as they worked for even more money. Or at least they had in Tess's family.

But Tess had found a balance in her life between what she needed and the money she had to live, and she intended to keep it that way.

Sure, she was a little on the shy side now, but things always evened out.

Tess hefted the duffel. It was heavy and would

definitely cause severe unevenness in her life. She'd been about to offer it all to Cat and Laine and Gracie, too, if she needed it, but these two had walked in before she'd had a chance.

She set the duffel at the kid's feet. "Here you go. I don't even know how much is in there. Just a lot."

"You misunderstand," Burned-Out One said. "We do want to talk to you about Henry, but the money is yours."

Were they nuts?

"Excuse me." The kid slid out of the booth and picked up the duffel, testing the weight. "A hundred big ones." He grinned at her. "You impressed him."

Cheeky kid. "You can tell how much there is from the weight?"

"I've had experience. He's done this before."

"Can he afford to?"

The two males exchanged a glance.

"I'll take that as a *yes*. But I'm still giving it back."

They stared at her.

"What?" She looked from one to the other.

"Sit." The drone pointed next to the kid and Tess sat, frankly surprised he had that much macho in him.

"Now, what are you drinking?" he asked.

Amused, she gestured with a nod. "My Cosmo is over on the bar."

Tess watched as he stood and walked over to the bar. Oh, yeah, she would have tipped him extra. He took a cocktail napkin, returned with her drink and set them carefully and correctly before her.

A customer waiting on her? This was a switch. "You've done this before."

The kid groaned. "We all do. I'm up next summer."

"Who is *we?*"

The man said, "I'm Evan McKenna and this is my cousin W—"

"Quatro Bartholomew." The kid gave Tess a smooth smile she knew he'd practiced in front of a mirror. "Henry is our great-uncle."

"I'm Tess. Henry is my best customer."

"I guess *so,*" the kid said.

"Not because of this." Tess kicked the duffel. "He's a regular. Comes in a few times a week, always asks for me, and tips great."

"I can see why." Quatro leered this time.

"W—Quatro," Evan warned quietly.

Tess's eyes narrowed as she caught the slip. "You know, you don't look like a Quatro."

"Have you ever met one?" the kid asked.

"No."

"Then I'll define Quatro for you. It'll be my pleasure. Maybe yours, too." He scooted a little closer and leered a little more.

Tess was in familiar territory here. What to do, what to do? There was such a fine line between a confidently sexy grin and a leer. The man-child needed to be taught the difference.

Evan made a low sound deep in his throat as he picked up his mug. It was both a warning and an acknowledgment of Quatro's impending doom.

Tess decided she liked the guy, not that she knew

him well enough, but she could size up people pretty quickly. This guy was dangerous because he was very appealing when he wasn't working. The problem was that his type was always working.

She may have underestimated the healing capabilities of Quatro's ego, though. While she'd been distracted by his cousin, he'd slid his arm across the back of the booth and was eyeing her.

"So—you got a boyfriend?" Quatro asked.

"No." Tess stared at his mouth and leaned forward, watching as his expression changed from confidence to hope to something resembling panic. "I'm not attracted to boys, kid."

She straightened as he visibly swallowed. "There you go, Evan," he said. "She's all yours."

"While I appreciate the gesture, Whitney might object."

Tess didn't need to ask who Whitney was. Clearly, she was either the girlfriend or the wife. So he was taken. All the good ones were.

Wait a minute. What was her problem? Evan may be good, but not for her. He was the type she avoided, so whether or not he was taken was nothing to her.

"Object? Get a clue, Evan. Whitney won't notice."

"You don't know what you're talking about."

"So when *was* the last time you saw your so-called girlfriend?"

"Can it, Woody."

"What's with the *Woody?*" Tess decided it was time to cool off the simmering testosterone.

"It was his nickname until recently," Evan told her.

"I like Woody." She looked at the kid who was chugging his Coke. "What's wrong with it?"

He swallowed. "Woody is 'that guy,' you know? The best friend, the chess club president, the water boy on the football team, the sidekick. Woody isn't the cool guy who gets the girl."

"It'll take a lot more than a name to get a girl," Tess said.

He hunched over his empty glass. "It's hard to explain. I act different as Quatro."

"Not an improvement," Tess told him. "Your moves smell like eau de jerk."

"That's cold." He looked wounded.

"Wouldn't you rather hear it from me than a girl you really liked?"

Evan chuckled before finishing off his beer.

Quatro looked across the table at his cousin. "How does Uncle Henry find them?"

"It's a gift." Evan stared at the bottom of the empty mug.

He was looking better. "Let me get you another one of those." Tess started to stand, but he shook his head.

"Later. We wanted—"

"Hang on," Tess interrupted him. "We've got to get your cousin's name straightened out. Okay, what's your real name?"

There was a telling silence.

"It can't be that bad."

Quatro drew a breath. "Elwood Phineas Bartholomew the Fourth." He inclined his head. "At your service."

"Oh, wow." Poor kid. "You know, there's a lot to work with there. What about Bart?"

"My dad grabbed that one."

Smart man. "Well, Phin is actually cool these days."

"Sounds like a shark. And it's my grandfather. My great-grandfather went by Elwood. You can just look at him and know he was never a Woody."

"Is he still alive?"

Quatro shook his head.

"Good news. Everybody moves up a number. You can be Trey."

"My family did not get the moving-up memo."

"Send them one, then," Tess told him.

"Right," he muttered.

"So…Quad." Even to Tess that one didn't sound good.

"A mutant muscle?"

"E.P.?"

He just looked at her.

She didn't even try E.B. "Well, can we combine parts of the names and come up with something like…?" She waved her hand as she thought.

"Elphin?" Evan offered with a straight face.

Tess snickered. "Too *Lord of the Rings*."

"Phinbar."

"Sounds like a sushi restaurant. Here's one—Barphin."

They both laughed and Tess learned that Evan did, indeed, know the difference between a leer and a sexy grin.

Lovely, but no. Pity, because Tess found herself at loose ends just now.

Woody/Quatro gave her an aggrieved look. "I hope you two are having a good time."

"Yes, Quatro, we are," Evan said.

They could have a lot better time if he were planning to stick around a while. But was she planning to stick around for much longer?

"So you agree that Quatro is my only option?"

"If that's what you want," Evan said.

Tess spoke up. "I still like Phin, and Woody isn't horrible, but so far I'm not liking the obnoxious aspects of the Quatro persona."

"I got that."

"Confidence is good. Sexy, even. But wallowing in it is like wearing too much cologne. Bad. You want to let chicks discover you all on their own. Think subtle."

"Nah." Quatro shook his head. "Evan is subtle. So subtle nobody ever notices him."

Tess glanced across the table where Quatro's cousin had relaxed against the back of the booth. Their eyes met. And held.

"Oh, honey, I noticed," she murmured.

2

He shouldn't be giving waitresses in small-town Texas bars looks like that.

But Tess was no ordinary waitress. There was the money-stuffed blue duffel, for one thing. There was the fact that she wanted nothing to do with it, for another.

She...interested him. Evan couldn't remember the last time a woman—or anything not connected to Bartholomew's Best—had interested him.

Tess had a practiced friendliness about her that Evan knew came with being dependent on tips. It hadn't come easily to him. He'd hated his summer of working in an Italian restaurant. Even now, he couldn't eat tomato-based pasta dishes. But Tess was either a natural or very experienced. Both, most likely.

She'd been great with Woody—Quatro. Some day, his cousin would appreciate it. Evan appreciated it now.

For the first time in hours, he didn't feel compelled to be doing anything other than what he was doing right now—sitting in a dark booth in a small-town chick pub as he contemplated ordering a second draft beer.

It was a nice place and clearly not doing the business it should. They needed a business plan. He could cook one up for them… *Not your responsibility.* Mentally backing away, he tuned in to the conversation.

Quatro was running off at the mouth and dumping their entire family history on the very patient Tess. He'd just finished telling her all about Uncle Henry and his penchant for giving money to ordinary but deserving people.

"Deserving?" She made a face. "That lets me out. I don't deserve anything."

"Henry must have thought so," Evan told her. "He likes his gifts to make a difference. Say, somebody who needs money to finish school. That's always popular. Or another favorite is the inventor."

"Oh, yeah," Quatro broke in. "He's funded more strange patents. And he likes people who've been working hard toward something—didn't he buy a fire engine for some town one time?"

"That doesn't count," Evan said. "He only did that so he could ride it in the Fourth of July parade."

"Self-serving and generous. I like it." Tess laughed, then sobered. "But I haven't invented anything and I'm not selling fire engines." She shook her head and nudged the duffel closer to Evan's side of the table.

He hadn't met many of the recipients of Henry's largesse, but to his knowledge, no one had ever refused the money before. "Sometimes, it's nothing more than a second chance." Evan knew about second chances.

"Ole Henry is pretty sharp," Quatro added. "He may not always be right, but he's never wrong."

Evan smiled to himself at hearing the oft-repeated description of their great-uncle.

"So what are y'all doing here?" Tess asked. "Do you track down everybody he gives money to?"

"No," Evan told her. "Uh, do you have time for us to go into this? I don't want to keep you from your work." Just because he suddenly found himself with nothing to do didn't mean others were in the same situation. Granted, he and his cousin were the only customers just now, but he didn't want to get her into trouble.

Tess glanced over toward the bar where the other women still talked together. "I've got time," she said. "You know, I don't think I've ever met anybody as polite as you."

Quatro made a rude noise. "You mean repressed."

"*I* was being polite." She grinned and Quatro laughed.

"Hey, it's like this," Quatro said. "Henry goes on vacation every year and makes everybody else take a vacation, too. Sometimes now, sometimes later. But Evan never gets around to taking his vacation. So this year, Henry locked him out."

"I have ongoing projects," Evan began. "I can't just—"

"Take a vacation from what?" Tess interrupted.

"Bartholomew's Best," Quatro answered. "Have you heard of it?"

"The department store? That big one in Austin?"

Quatro nodded. Evan wasn't sure he wanted to parade all the family issues before her, but there was something about Tess. Something that Henry had clearly responded to.

Something that Evan was responding to. Sitting here, the knot in his stomach had eased somewhat. Sure, the beer helped, but the whole atmosphere affected him. Talking to Tess was relaxing. It could be addictive, if he'd let it.

"Yeah, I've heard of Bartholomew's Best." She didn't look impressed. "Expensive."

"Because it carries only the best," Quatro said at the same time Evan said, "You get what you pay for."

"We carry only one type of each item," he continued. "The top-rated in the field. Sometimes that changes because we constantly test and evaluate."

Tess held up both hands. "I wasn't criticizing. I'm just saying that not everyone can afford the best."

"It's actually cheaper in the long run," Evan began. How many times had he made this same argument? It was kind of funny to see Quatro nodding his head in agreement. As soon as they were old enough to understand it, everybody in the family passionately believed in the Bartholomew's Best corporate culture: never accept less than the best. Henry extended it to personnel. If employees gave their best workday, then they shouldn't be required to give overtime.

Except Evan was currently having trouble with the vacation policy, but he was working on that.

"If Bartholomew's Best carries an item, it will last

years," he told Tess. "You buy, say, a set of tools or pots and pans and you can pass them down to your grandchildren and they'll be as good as new. They won't wear out and have to be replaced, so longevity justifies the initial higher cost."

"Yeah, well, if you've only got forty-nine ninety-five in your budget for a set of pots and pans, instead of the nine hundred those fancy French things cost, then you end up with cheapies."

"We have layaway," Quatro said.

"Layaway." She rolled her eyes. "So what do I cook dinner in tonight while my pots and pans are in layaway? Huh?"

Actually, Evan was working on the cost issue, which surveys indicated was a growing concern, but would anybody listen to him? No. And after three weeks away, he'd lose what little momentum he had.

When Quatro didn't answer her, Tess turned to Evan. "So you're locked out and you want to hassle Henry into letting you back in."

"That's about it."

Tess stared at him. Evan hoped she had a clue where Henry was going and was trying to decide whether to tell him. He tried to look trustworthy and nonthreatening.

"You need a vacation," she said.

"Why does everyone keep telling me that?"

"Maybe it's the dark circles under your eyes, the pasty skin, the nervous tic—"

"I do not have a nervous tic."

"You might as well."

Quatro hooted. "Give it up, Evan. She's got your number."

"I—" A complete stranger—an attractive complete stranger—had just told him he looked like hell.

Well, maybe he did. And sure, maybe he could use a break, but now wasn't the time. He said so.

"For your type, it's never the time," Tess said.

"My type?" It was the dismissive tone that got to him.

"The classic type A workaholic. The kind who never exercises." She looked him up and down and checked under the table. "You're not too far gone, but you will be in ten years. Your job is everything to you, and your family, if you've got one, comes second. Always. You tell yourself they don't understand that you have to work hard so they can enjoy their wonderful lifestyle. You miss birthdays, school plays, concerts, anniversaries, parties, graduations, always telling yourself that you'll be there next time. And you mean it. Only next time never comes and there you are, fifty-six years old and carrying fifty extra pounds, with high blood pressure, soaring cholesterol and a jumbo-sized bottle of antacids. You eat on the run, so it's understandable that you have heartburn. Only it isn't heartburn. It's angina. And one day, a day when you're irritated with everyone because you aren't feeling too good, but you still dragged yourself into work and went to a meeting only to find that the idiots under you haven't produced the all-important whatever you're currently producing—you get really mad. So you yell at them.

And you walk out into the hallway, clutch your chest, stumble into your office and shut the door so no one can see you. And then you die." She gulped two quick breaths. "And you lie there until your twenty-year-old daughter, who's interning with your company because it's the only way she can see her dad—finds you."

Evan gazed at Tess. She gazed back, breathing rapidly. Had she really just described his future? Or had she just described her past?

"Wow," Quatro said into the silence.

"You weren't talking hypothetically, were you, Tess?" Evan asked.

"No." She took another breath, waited, then breathed deeply and stood. "So take your vacation, Evan. Take a lot of vacations. Go out to dinner with what's her name. Have a nice life." She bent and dragged the duffel from the floor to the bench next to Quatro. Unzipping the thing, she said, "Henry took the bottle of cognac with him—I don't mind, but it was still half full and, well, I'm going to take three hundred dollars to cover the cost. That's wholesale. I know Temptation's owners would just say to forget it, but they can't afford to."

They all looked at the stacks of money. Tess picked one up and pulled out three hundred-dollar bills.

"Tess, Henry meant for you to have that money." Evan didn't understand why she didn't want it. It was there. She didn't have to do anything.

"No." She seemed agitated, which didn't fit with

her I-can-take-anything-the-world-can-throw-at-me attitude.

"No matter what you think, Henry gives it to deserving people."

"Evan, you shouldn't have put it that way," Quatro said. "Henry gives money to people he wants to have money. What did he say to you, Tess?"

"Nothing, but there was a note." She zipped the bag, then dug in a side pocket. "I put it in here. I guess I should write him a note back, huh? Oh." She pulled out two envelopes, looked at them, and then smiled widely. "'Tess, you may encounter my great-nephew, Evan,'" she read. "'If you do, will you please give him this and tell him to take a chill pill?'" She gave a crack of laughter and handed Evan the note.

"I hate it when he tries to talk cool," Quatro mumbled.

Evan stared at the envelope before ripping into it. Was he that predictable?

Apparently so.

"What's it say?" Quatro asked.

Mentally grumbling, Evan read, "'Evan, stop trying to find me. I don't want to be found and I wouldn't let you continue to work yourself into the ground even if you did find me. You need a break. A long one, but a few weeks will have to do. When I get back, if I am not convinced that you are rested and refreshed, I will extend your vacation until such time as I am convinced of your return to good and strong mental health. And you know I will.'"

"He would," Quatro said.

"Sounds like he knows you pretty well," Tess commented, her eyes accusing him of being a workaholic like her father.

Evan thought about what she'd said. Thought about how her eyes looked when they weren't accusatory, too. Contemplated the fact that if he had to go back to work tomorrow, he'd never see Tess again and her eyes would haunt him.

"Okay, so I'm on vacation." He threw up his hands. "Now what? I didn't have time to plan anything. June is prime vacation time. Mr. and Mrs. America and their two-point-four children are clogging the highways and byways, not to mention flights to Cancun."

Quatro nudged his arm. "There's more writing on the back."

Evan flipped over the sheet of paper.

"'You weren't supposed to plan anything. Do nothing. Just be.'"

"What is he, psychic?" Quatro asked.

"He's sounding a little New Age for me." Evan imagined just *being*. "I'll be crazy, that's what I'll be." He looked down at the letter and laughed when he read the next line. "'Or go fishing. Same thing.' I hate fishing."

"Keep reading." Quatro pointed. "I see Tess's name."

"What does he say about me?" Tess asked.

"'If you're still at a loss, I suggest you observe Tess and watch her follow her dream. Maybe you'll learn something.'"

"Oh, great. He wants me to be a highly paid baby-sitter."

Evan smiled at her disgusted face. "What's your dream, Tess?"

"No." She shook her head. "Forget it."

"It can't be much of a dream, then."

Still shaking her head, she walked a couple of steps from the table, then strode back. "He wants me to go to Nashville and launch a singing career. This—" she waved a hand at the duffel "—was supposed to be money to rent a studio so I could cut a demo."

Quatro sat up. "Nashville. Hey, Evan, we could do Nashville. Road trip! I'll drive."

"No."

It was Tess who'd spoken. Oddly, Evan was finding the idea of a trip to Nashville in a limo with Tess a very good idea. "Let's do it," he said.

"Whoa." Quatro looked at him as though Evan had grown horns.

"That's probably the first spontaneous decision you've ever made, isn't it?" Tess asked.

"Pretty much," he admitted. It felt good. It felt reckless. He gazed at Tess and felt a warmth gathering below his belly. It felt sexy.

"Too bad it isn't happening."

"Tess—"

There was an interesting expression on her face and Evan thought he might have convinced her when she yelled, "Hey Laine—fire up the karaoke!"

The three women at the bar froze. "Are you sure?" one of them asked.

She arched an eyebrow at Evan. "I'm in a Whitney mood."

There was a collective groan. "Not 'I Will Always Love You'?"

"Oh, yeah."

"What are they drinking?" called the woman behind the bar.

"I'll get it." Tess brought Evan another beer and some peanuts and a Coke for Quatro. "The crunch helps," she said, inexplicably.

Okay, so maybe it was time for another beer and some good music. Evan took a long swallow as he watched Tess stroll toward a small stage that was now lit up.

She did have a good stroll. She stepped up to the stage, flashed a little more leg, and straddled the microphone as the first notes of music filled the place.

Things were definitely heating up. She looked as though she owned the stage. She also looked right at him. Evan's mouth went dry, so he drank some more.

"We just gotta talk her into going to Nashville," Quatro murmured.

Yeah, Nashville was sounding mighty fine. Evan was thinking of his enforced vacation in an entirely new light. Good ole Uncle Henry.

The spotlight shone down and gleamed off her brown hair. She had good hair. Good everything. Evan thought about twenty-year-old Tess finding her father on the floor. She'd told him the story to warn him. Uncle Henry had warned him. Even his cousin, who normally thought the world revolved around himself, thought he needed time off.

But did he have to take a vacation now?

Tess closed her eyes and swayed sensuously to a rhythm all her own. One Evan suddenly wanted to join. Okay, now was good for a vacation. What were his chances of convincing Tess to take one with him?

Talk about spontaneous. That should please everybody. Except maybe Whitney, but he was having trouble remembering exactly what Whitney looked like just now. She didn't have gleaming straight brown hair and she sure didn't wear her skirts that short and while he knew she wore boots sometimes, they didn't look like Tess's boots. And she didn't walk like Tess or throw back her head and laugh like Tess and she'd never be caught dead on a karaoke stage...

Tess was saying something—no, that was the beginning of the song. She was doing kind of a talksing. She had a husky sexy voice, just as he knew she would. A woman couldn't look the way Tess looked and not have a sexy voice.

And then the music swelled with the familiar chorus. "*IIIIIIIIIIIIIIIeeeeeeIIIIIIIIIII—*"

Goose bumps prickled Evan's arms as his blood ran cold. He gulped his beer and gritted his teeth.

His cousin gripped his arm. "Evan?"

"She's nervous."

Quatro grabbed for the peanuts. He ate one, shell and all. After the next chorus, Evan joined him.

"Youuuuuuuuuuuuuuohhhhhheeeeohhhhhuuuu-uuuuu—"

Quatro leaned over. "Was that yodeling?"

"It sounds like she's trying to find the melody."

"She will never find the melody. She is not even in the same hemisphere as the melody."

Evan braced himself for the chorus.

"YouuuuuuuuuuuuueeeewwwwwUUUUUUUU-UUUUUooooooooo—"

She was chasing the melody through multiple octaves. It outran her. The pang in Evan's molar returned and there was a metallic taste in his mouth. And he was out of beer.

He looked around, only to find the bartender already headed his way. She set another beer in front of him and brought more peanuts. "Drinks are half price when Tess sings."

"Does she…?"

"Know she's bad? Yeah, but secretly, I don't think she believes it." The bartender gave Evan a sympathetic smile before walking off.

Tess wasn't just bad. Tess redefined bad. Tess's voice would cause prison riots. Actually, Evan could see some military possibilities. Enemy holed up somewhere? Play a recording of Tess singing "I Will Always Love You" and they'd surrender without a shot being fired.

"Evan, make her stop," whimpered Quatro.

"YouuuuuuueeeeeuuuuuuuIiiiiiEEEEEEEEiiiiii—"

"Just a little longer. I think this is the big finish," Evan told him.

"Of her or us?"

After some more warbling, as though she needed to test every sound possible for the human voice to make—and some he hadn't thought it was possible to make—the music faded away. Tess's singing stopped shortly afterward.

"Is it possible that the money was a bribe for her to never sing again?" Evan wondered aloud.

"She's coming toward us. What do we say?" Quatro whispered.

"As little as possible. But be positive."

"I am positive that was the worst singing I've ever heard."

Tess sat right back down and clasped her hands on the table. "Well?" she asked brightly, clearly pleased with herself. She did look pretty with her cheeks flushed.

Her heart had been in her singing. At this point, Evan was prepared to overlook the fact that her voice hadn't been. He mustered all the enthusiasm of which he was capable. "That was *incredible*."

"Really?" Her eyes sparkled.

Henry, I'm right with you on this. "Oh, yeah."

"How about you?" she asked Quatro. "What did you think?"

"It was sure something else." He shook his head. "And I mean that."

Tess looked from one to the other. "So…does tone deafness run in your family, then?"

This was a test, one of those situations fate liked

to throw his way occasionally. Evan hoped fate was amused.

"What do you mean?" Quatro asked carefully.

His cousin had clearly encountered these little life tests as well.

Tess studied Quatro. "Are you and Evan tone-deaf like your uncle?"

"Uncle Henry's tone-deaf?" Quatro looked at Evan.

"It's never come up in conversation," he said.

"I'm not tone-deaf," Quatro told Tess.

Tess tilted the peanut bowl and looked at the table. "Where are the shells?"

"Ate 'em."

Tess smiled. "So you're being sweet!"

"Is that a good thing?" Quatro asked.

"It's very good. It means there's hope for the Quatro persona." Tess leveled a look at Evan. "Is there hope for you?"

Evan could be sweet, too. "You looked great on the stage," he told her.

"And my singing?"

A direct question wasn't fair. "Don't singers lip-synch in performances these days? I think it's all about appearance. And let me just emphasize that you have nailed appearance."

"You sure are a squiggly one to pin down. There's hope for you, too." She grinned. "I love to sing. When I was up there, I sounded just like Whitney Houston—better than Whitney Houston. However, enough people have told me I can't sing that I believe them—except Henry. He's the only other person I've met who thinks I can sing. I told him I can't, but he doesn't believe me. All he sees is how happy my singing makes the people in the bar. Everybody cheers and smiles and carries on. And you know why?"

"Because you look *really* good on the stage?"

"Because drinks are half price when I sing."

Quatro made a muffled sound, but Evan just laughed. And laughed. Deep, relaxing laughter. And when he tried to stop, because it had to be insulting to Tess, he couldn't, which made the others laugh, too.

"So you see, I can't take the money," she said.

"Tough. You've got it." Frankly, he thought she'd earned it.

"Here's an idea." Quatro set down his Coke. "If Uncle Henry wants a CD, then we can make one for him ourselves."

The recording equipment would probably break first, Evan thought.

"Oh, come on," Tess said.

"No, see, you just sing into my computer microphone and I'll burn a CD. It won't cost anything and you can give it to Uncle Henry. You'll still have all your money. We live in Austin, so it's just a couple of hours from here. Or actually, anybody with a computer could do it for you."

TESS CONSIDERED IT and felt a heavy weight settle on her shoulders. "I don't want the money."

"Now see, this is the part I don't get," Quatro said.

"Why don't you want the money?" Evan asked.

"It's too much trouble." She didn't expect him to understand. Most people wouldn't unless they'd experienced firsthand how easy it was to get used to having money and then wanting more. "It's a lot of responsibility. Responsibility isn't my thing."

"Tess, if you're worried about how to handle it, I can help you. You can invest the money and then you can forget about it until you need it. There are people out there who make a living managing other people's money."

Look at him, getting all stressed at the thought of her with all that money. No, she didn't need it. She did like the idea of making the CD with Quatro, though.

A buzz sounded. Evan made a face and grabbed his cell phone. "Finally, somebody calling me back."

As Tess watched, all his lovely mellowness evaporated. He'd been looking good and she'd liked the way he'd stared at her while she was on the stage. Usually, she couldn't see much past the colored stage lights, but there was still enough ambient light in the bar that she could see Evan and Quatro.

She wondered about his so-called girlfriend, because there was a lot of hunger in the way he looked at her. Hunger she wouldn't mind feeding.

And the way he looked now, all stressed and pinched, made her want to use his uncle's money to lure Evan over to the dark side of fun and irresponsibility.

And why not? It could be fun. She checked on the group over by the bar. They didn't need her now.

And, truthfully, she had no say in what they decided to do with the bar. Those three had been friends long before she had ever got here and though they'd included her in their circle, she was still an outsider.

But an outsider with money. She stood, grabbed the empty peanut bowl, swiped at the table and cleared the glasses. Then she headed straight for the women by the bar.

"Hey." She thunked the dirty glasses on the rubber tray behind the bar.

"Hey," Cat said back at her. "You know those guys?"

"Nah." Tess looked over her shoulder at Evan and Quatro. Both were talking on cell phones. "They're relatives of Henry's."

"So they want the money back?" Laine asked.

Tess shook her head. "No, they just wanted to know where Henry went. So listen, if you and Cat, or Gracie, need the money to buy another bar, or something, you're welcome to it."

They didn't react the way Tess thought they would. She kind of expected relieved smiles and pats on the back and a little Tess-as-heroine scenario. Wasn't happening. Maybe they were still numb from learning the bar would have to close.

"Tess," Cat began.

"We can't take your money," Laine said.

"I don't want it. And there's a lot there." She looked at Gracie, who had been silent.

"I'm thinking, I'm thinking," she said. "You know, I've got this reunion coming up. I could make quite a splash with all that money."

"Gracie." Laine shook her head.

"I was just kidding," Gracie said. "Sort of."

The others laughed half-heartedly.

Tess figured pride wouldn't let them accept the money, but she'd offered. And truth to tell, she was sort of hurt that they wouldn't accept help from her.

Maybe that's the way Henry would feel when he found out she'd given back the money. It was something to consider.

She looked back at Evan and Quatro. More at Evan. In thirty years, he'd be her father. Maybe less.

"At least you don't have to worry about paying me," she told Cat and Laine. And I know, well…" She gestured at the nearly empty bar.

"If you weren't working here, where would you go?" Laine asked her.

"Austin," Tess decided immediately, the way she always had.

"Then go ahead and take off," Cat told her. "I don't know how long we'll keep Temptation open."

And clearly, Tess wasn't going to be a part of the last days. The thought bothered her more than she'd admit to anyone, even herself. She was the outsider. It wasn't her problem.

Fine. She'd go to Austin, then. She nodded at Cat. "Let me know if you get in a jam."

"How? You don't have a cell phone."

"I'll check in when I've got a number."

"You can afford a cell phone now," Gracie said.

"I don't like being interrupted when I'm living my life," Tess told her. "Look, you guys have been

great. I've stayed here longer than I've stayed anywhere. I'm going to miss you."

They all sniffed and nodded. Tess liked to think
that they were tearing up at the thought of her leaving, but figured it was the situation in general. Her
own eyes stung, which was just stupid.

She let everyone hug her and didn't even mind it.
Then she went back to the booth.

"Hey," she said to Quatro, as Evan punched a finger into his ear and stood up to pace so he could hear
his cell phone better. "Is that CD offer still open?"

"Sure," Quatro said.

"I, uh…" Tess hated making plans. "Look, this
place is going to shut down 'cause of the road construction and I'll be taking off. I'd like to make a CD
for Henry before I go."

"And then what?"

"And then I don't know."

He gazed at her, weighing something, and Tess got
a glimpse of the man he would become. Same genetic
pool as Evan and Henry. There was good stuff there.

Finally, Quatro nodded imperceptibly toward
Evan. "You…make him relax. He needs that."

They both watched Evan get tense and hunched
and pinched and wound tighter and tighter. The
muscle in his jaw was getting quite a workout. What
a waste of man.

"He looks like he's about to blow a gasket," Tess
said.

"You think maybe you could stick around Austin
for a while?"

"And help your cousin chill?"

Quatro nodded. "He can help you figure out what to do with the money. It'll keep his mind off Bartholomew's Best."

This had actually been along the lines of what Tess had been thinking. "But you don't even know me."

"I know enough. And Henry knows you."

"From bar conversation? I don't think so."

"You'd be surprised at what Henry knows."

"Hey!" Evan held the phone from his ear and stared at it. "A summer *intern* just hung up on me!" Almost frantically, he thumbed a phone number and raked his other hand through his hair.

"He needs help now," Tess said. "I've got the time—and I've sure got the money." She grinned. "This could be some serious fun."

3

GREAT THINGS HAD HAPPENED while he was on the phone. Not his conversation with the assistants of people who wouldn't take his calls—that wasn't great. Or the assistants, themselves, who ultimately wouldn't take his calls, even when he had information that couldn't wait...

Forget relaxation techniques. Evan opened the limo's window and watched Tess's faded blue car lurch toward her house—now there was a transmission on its way out—and felt himself unwind.

Somehow, Quatro had convinced her to come to Austin *right now* and the thought that he was going to see her again made him feel...happy? Maybe more anticipatory in a good way. A sexy way, if he were being honest. In a way he did not feel with Whitney anymore, if he were being even more honest.

He should stop analyzing and just go with it. Tess, with her long legs and her bad singing and her crooked smile, had become very important to him in a very short time.

He wasn't going to analyze that, either.

The plan was that Tess was going to pack and follow them to Austin, stop off at his cousin's house and make the CD. It was a good plan. A fabulous plan. Evan smiled to himself as they pulled into the driveway of a duplex.

"Stay here," he told his cousin. Not that Quatro hadn't been particularly helpful, but Evan wanted to talk to Tess without an audience.

She was waiting for him by the door.

"I'm going to pay my rent, thanks to your uncle. I should give notice, too, since I can't see myself hanging around this town now that Temptation is a goner."

She sure did make snap decisions. "Where are you going to go?"

"To Austin with you." She gave him a surprised look as she rang the doorbell.

"I know that, but then what?"

"Stay a while."

Evan's heart kicked up a notch. "Just like that?"

"I like Austin. You aren't the only person who lives there."

After that deflating remark, the door opened and Evan found himself in a modest kid-friendly suburban home.

"Hey, Madison," Tess said to the preteen blond girl who'd opened the door.

"Mom!" the girl yelled.

"It's me, Mary Alice," Tess called.

A frazzled-mom type dried her hands on a kitchen towel as she came into the room. She barely glanced at him.

"This is Evan." Tess hooked a thumb toward him.

After a tight acknowledging smile, the woman raised her eyebrows at Tess.

"I want to talk to you about the rent," Tess began.

Mary Alice closed her eyes. "Oh, Tess."

"What?" Tess looked baffled.

"Mom?"

The woman clasped the girl to her. "I know business hasn't been good at the bar, but if you could pay *anything* it would help. I mean, there's last month, too, and I had to pay the mortgage and it didn't leave enough cash to make the early registration deadline for Girl Scout camp."

Tess's mouth worked. "You should have said something."

She hadn't quite spluttered, but Evan could tell that she was completely thrown by her landlady's reaction.

"Well, Madison can still go if I pay a late fee, but the money is due in by the end of the week and now…"

"I'm not going to get to go to camp, am I?" Madison sounded very calm. Very much as though she'd been disappointed like this before.

Evan wondered if he should leave, but found himself fascinated by Tess's reaction. She'd been so adamant about not taking Henry's money that she hadn't realized she needed it.

"I'm here to *pay*." Tess scrambled for her purse, a big beat up leather satchel thing. "But I wondered if it was okay to give you cash." She pulled out one of Uncle Henry's bundles.

Mary Alice's eyes widened. She cleared her throat. "Cash is good."

"Okay, then." Tess's cheeks were flushed. She peeled off a few bills. "Here's last month's rent, here's this month's, and here's a month in lieu of notice."

"Notice?" Mary Alice stared at her palm as Tess laid bills across it.

"Yeah, I'm heading to Austin. In fact, here's another month because I don't have time to clean the place. Sorry."

"Is that real money?" Madison asked. "That's Benjamin Franklin, isn't it?"

"Uh-huh." Tess nodded.

"Tess, the security deposit is only—"

"Mary Alice, let me do this. Who knows how long it'll take you to find a new tenant? Also, here's money for the late fee for camp."

Mary Alice tried to give it back. "It's not that much."

"The rest is interest because I was late. I—you really should have bugged me. I could have given you some money. I didn't realize it was crucial—"

"How did you think I was going to pay the mortgage?" Mary Alice snapped.

It was clear to Evan that Tess hadn't thought. Talk about clueless, though he hadn't thought her the clueless type.

"Here's more because I need a favor." Tess peeled off additional bills.

"Tess, stop it."

"No, really. I'm going to pack some of my stuff to

take with me, but if you could store the rest of it until I get back here, I'd appreciate it."

"Yeah, sure." Mary Alice stared at the money in her palm, then sent such a suspicious look at Evan that he took a step back. "This money isn't…" Instead of finishing she glanced down at her daughter.

Evan had no idea what she was thinking, but it couldn't be good. "Tess won…an award given out by my uncle."

The woman still looked suspicious.

"For her singing career," Evan added.

"Okay, now I know something's off." Mary Alice tried to hand back the money.

Here was someone who had heard Tess sing. "My uncle is, uh, tone-deaf. But he appreciates enthusiasm."

Tess began laughing. "It's okay, Mary Alice. He won't take the money back. He's nuts."

"Hey," Evan said.

"And Henry is tone-deaf. Anyway, Evan is going to help me handle the money and I'm going to handle Evan." She grasped his arm and kind of melted against him. Evan felt his skin warm through the material of his shirt and forgave her for the nuts remark.

Mary Alice cleared her throat and gestured to her daughter.

"Mom!" Madison sounded disgusted. "You ought to see what's on MTV."

"That wasn't a good strategic comeback," Evan murmured.

"Maybe I *should* see what's on MTV," was the ominous response.

"I'm going to go pack," Tess told them. "I'll stop by when I'm ready to leave."

Evan and Tess backed out before the mother-daughter exchange escalated.

Tess pulled away from him as soon as the door closed behind them. She gazed straight ahead as they walked to the other side of the duplex. "Don't say anything."

He glanced down at her. "I wasn't going to." Not when he hoped for more warm Tess pressed against him in the future.

"You don't have to. It was that look you gave me. And you don't know me well enough to look at me like that."

"Like what?"

"Like making me feel guilty because I haven't paid my rent."

"And why haven't you paid your rent?"

"See? See?" She opened the door of a barely furnished space and headed toward the bedroom without looking to see if Evan was behind her.

He was behind her all right. The lack of furnishings and anything remotely personal told him more about Tess than she realized. This woman was not the commitment type.

"Okay, I assume you didn't pay the rent because you didn't have the money." Evan leaned against the wall just inside the doorway. It seemed safest.

Tess yanked open a drawer. "I forgot, okay? And then I spent the money because I thought I'd already paid the rent and when I remembered that I hadn't,

I didn't have money anymore, but I figured I'd make it up in tips, only I didn't."

"Oh," Evan said.

"Don't you say 'oh' to me like that!"

This was one of those times when silence was his best bet. Okay with him. It was more fun to watch her anyway. Tess was emptying drawers into a garbage bag. Evan had never seen anything like it outside of summer camp. After knotting the end of the bag, she peeled off her pillowcase and disappeared into the bathroom.

Wincing as he heard plastic, glass, and who knew what jumble together, Evan stayed put.

Moments later, Tess emerged and set the pillowcase next to the trash bag. "I didn't know Mary Alice lived that close to the edge, okay?" She marched over to the closet and knocked a leopard-print suitcase down from the top shelf. "She should have said something." Tess unzipped the suitcase, squeezed an armful of clothes together and lifted them off the rod. Then she stuffed them, hangers and all, into the suitcase. "I mean, how was I supposed to know?"

She fascinated him and, at the risk of incurring her wrath, he was going to answer. "I know you're an anti-responsibility free spirit, but you made a commitment to pay rent. When you don't keep your commitments, people suffer. I don't think that's the lesson Henry wanted me to learn, though."

Tess sat on her suitcase and worked the zipper closed between her legs. This maneuver also fascinated Evan, especially as it revealed more than her fair share of leg. He didn't know a woman's legs could be that long.

"I should give Henry's money to Mary Alice." She looked up at him and beamed. "That's what I'll do!"

Evan shook his head. "She won't take it."

"I'll just leave it."

"Tess…" He shook his head.

"You're probably right." Tess looked momentarily deflated. "Guess I'll have to spend it on project Loosen Up Evan, then."

Evan started to tell her that there was no obligation for her to spend her money on him when he realized exactly what she'd said. "I'm plenty loose. I'm also responsible. Do not mistake responsibility for uptightness."

She wound her legs together, hooking her foot behind her ankle. Evan had a passing thought about limberness before he caught the expression on her face.

"You are winched tighter than a new belt on all-you-can-eat fajita night."

Certain things were wound and it was not from overwork. "I am not."

She gazed up at him from beneath her lashes. The temperature in the room rose. Her legs unwound and, with a liquid motion, she pushed herself off the suitcase.

He took an involuntary step back and she smiled. "Oh…yes…you…are." With each word, she walked toward him until she invaded his personal space and it was either step back or be run over.

His heart hammered and he felt the wall at his back.

And she still undulated forward until she was as close as she could be without actually touching him.

He felt the heat of her body. He could smell her scent—a little smoke, a little citrus and a lot of warm woman.

He held himself rigidly away from her, afraid to breathe too deeply in case he touched her and unwound all over her.

His eyes followed hers as she studied his face.

He may have bitten his tongue.

She poked the center of his chest with her finger and he flinched. "Tight. Very tight." And then she stepped away and dragged her suitcase off the bed as though nothing had happened. "You have *got* to relax."

He'd been more relaxed before that little display. "I guess I've forgotten how. I—I try visualization. You know, ocean and waves." Could he possibly sound like more of a dork? "It doesn't work, though."

"Of course it doesn't work." She passed by him rolling her suitcase. "You need sex and lots of it. Grab those bags for me, will you?"

Tess wished she'd been able to see Evan's face, but that would have spoiled the effect.

Girlfriend, ha. Tess wanted to meet this so-called girlfriend. She didn't poach, but this man was looking more and more like fair game to her.

She didn't say anything to Evan as they loaded her car. She wanted him thinking all the way to Austin.

But when she started her car, it lurched and then, engine still running, wouldn't go.

Evan and Quatro circled back. "Transmission," they chorused from beneath her hood.

"Is that bad?" Tess asked.

"Expensive," Quatro said. "Not to mention the other stuff."

"Other stuff?" But she kinda sorta suspected there was lots of other stuff.

"That car isn't worth fixing," Evan told her. "You can afford to buy a new one. A *safe* one."

She could. And since she was headed who knows where, reliable transportation would be a good thing. "Yeah, I can see myself in a new car," Tess said. "A convertible." Reliable didn't have to be stodgy.

Quatro's eyes lit up. "Let me go shopping with you."

"I'll take Tess car shopping," Evan said.

"Tess won't like your kind of cars." Quatro hauled her bags to the limo's trunk.

"She won't be looking for your kind, either." Evan carried her suitcase. It seemed she was going to ride with them. Tess was okay with that.

After telling Mary Alice about her car, making arrangements to have it hauled away and saying goodbye, Tess found herself in the lap of luxury. Her family had been well-off, but they'd never had a limo.

"You know, it's frightening how easy I could get used to this," she murmured as she stroked the limo's leather seat.

"Yeah." It came out as a strangled croak.

When Tess looked up at him, she found Evan's

eyes trained on the movements of her hand, which, coincidentally or not, happened to be really close to an expanse of fishnetted leg above her boots.

She smiled and Evan blinked.

"Head on out, Quatro," he said.

And just like that, Tess left Kendall, Texas, her home for the past two years.

Tess had a feeling that the limo ride would have been a lot more fun if Quatro had closed the privacy glass, but he didn't and Evan didn't ask him to and Tess didn't want the corruption of a minor on her conscience, so she didn't mention it. As things turned out, the ride was a lot of fun anyway.

HE WAS AWARE of her. Of everything about her. If Evan didn't know better, he'd swear she'd put something in his drink. Just hours ago, getting back into Bartholomew's Best corporate headquarters had been the most important thing on his mind. Now, he wasn't sure he had much of a mind left.

Hooking up with a stranger was not at all his style, but it was Henry's. Maybe he'd inherited something from the Bartholomew side of the family, after all.

He could talk to Tess—and did—and was fascinated by the life she'd been living since her father's death.

He and Quatro told her Henry stories and he laughed so much his abs were sore. She laughed, too, a deep uninhibited laughter.

By the time they arrived on the outskirts of Austin, he was in serious lust for her. She was prime vacation-fling material, that's what she was. She didn't like to stay too long in one place—no responsibilities, no strings, no commitments and maybe even no underwear. He couldn't remember if he'd seen any falling from the drawers she'd emptied.

It wasn't like him to contemplate things like whether the woman he was with was wearing underwear.

Was he having a nervous breakdown? He'd turned off his cell phone. Or rather, Tess had, but he'd let her.

Tess reached out and pressed a finger between his eyebrows. "Relax. Close your eyes."

He did.

"You're in a car. A car with soft leather interior and a great suspension. Someone else is driving. There's nothing else you have to be doing right now but riding in the car. Worrying is counterproductive because it expends mental energy and exacts a toll on your body. The most productive activity for you right now is to relax and recharge."

Her fingers massaged slow circles against his temples and her voice combined with the hum of the car soothed him.

His mind emptied until there was only Tess— maybe wearing underwear, maybe not.

"You live here all by yourself?" Tess dropped the blue duffel in the middle of Evan's living room.

"Yes."

"Why?" she asked.

"Well, this property became available, and the

schools are ranked highest and the crime rate the lowest. The builder is known for quality, and the area should continue to appreciate."

As he spoke, Tess walked down the hallway toward his bedroom, stuck her head in, and then headed upstairs.

"You have four bedrooms and a playroom and...a big closet?"

"Media room."

Tess peered down at him from the balcony overlooking the two-story foyer. "You have a media room with no media in it."

"I haven't gotten around to buying the equipment yet. The Bartholomew's research team hasn't rated HD plasma screen TVs yet."

"Oh, well, then." She came down the stairs and though he shamelessly looked up, he still couldn't answer the underwear thing.

"Why, Evan, are you looking up my skirt?"

"Yeah."

She stopped right in front of him and grinned. "Trying to see my underpants?"

"If there are any to see." This was way past bold for him.

"Working in a bar in a skirt this short? Please." She walked past him. "Though I am encouraged that you're interested."

Before he could think of anything to say, she breezed on. "Now, what is with you and all this space? You aren't using it. I mean, one of the upstairs bedrooms is completely empty. Another has some dusty exercise equipment and another looks like a teen girl's room. What's with that?"

"Jocelyn—Quatro's sister. It was, uh, her room. She outgrew that stuff and redecorated, so I took all the furniture."

"A girl's room." Tess leveled a look at him. "Were you married or something?"

Evan shook his head. "But some day I plan to be, and I didn't want to let this property get away."

"Whitney?"

"What about her?"

"Did she talk you into buying this place?"

"No. She was out of the country when I bought this place."

Tess eyed him. "Is she still out of the country?"

"No."

"Evan, is she your girlfriend or isn't she?"

"Yes." He hesitated. "I think so."

"Buddy, if you have to think about it, then you don't have a girlfriend." Tess waved around. "I don't see any evidence of girlfriend encroachment."

"Huh?"

"No plants, no wreaths, no decorative pillows, no accessories."

"I like a clean, contemporary style."

"This isn't contemporary, this is bachelor I-don't-care. And if you had a girlfriend, then she would have put little markers in here."

"What do you mean?"

"The stuff that tells other women, like me, that you're taken."

Evan looked around his living area. He had a black leather couch and a chrome coffee table, a matching recliner, a TV and a swing-arm lamp. "I guess I could use a couple of pillows."

"Has Whitney seen this place?"

Tess had unknowingly—or maybe knowingly—hit on a sore spot. "She's only been back a little while and is still adjusting. Jet lag," he added lamely.

"Oh." Tess looked startled. "When did she get back?"

There was a brief silence. "February."

More silence and then Tess held up her fingers and ticked them off. "March, April, May, June. Four months. Four. I've never heard of a case of jet lag lasting four months."

"We dated and her job took her to London for two years."

Tess's eyes widened. "Let me guess. You were faithful all that time."

"Of course!"

Smiling faintly, she touched his shoulder. Warmth and awareness radiated from the spot. "For some men, there is no *of course*. You buried yourself in your work, didn't you?"

"I suppose I did. I hadn't thought."

"You *have* seen her since she got back, right?"

He nodded, thinking of the disastrous dinner. "She said she needed time." Why was he telling Tess all this?

"She's had plenty of time," Tess told him. "We're going to deal with her later."

"We?"

"You betcha. Okay, I'm hungry and Quatro was making dinner noises. Potluck at his house. Help me unload my stuff and let's get going."

"Unload your..." But Tess was headed out his front door. "Tess!" he called after her. She didn't respond. He caught up to her just as she and Quatro popped the limo's trunk. "You can't stay here!"

Both of them looked surprised. "It's not like you don't have the room. You're swimming in room. Why should I waste your uncle's money on a hotel when you've got all that room?"

Evan watched her bend over to retrieve her garbage bag of clothes and knew that no amount of room would be enough with Tess staying under the same roof.

4

HOME. THAT WAS TESS'S first thought as she stood in the immense foyer of the Bartholomew manse. She already knew that Henry occupied the "mother-in-law" wing and that Quatro, his parents, his sister and the odd cousin or two occupied the rest of the house.

Tess knew they'd all be surprised to learn that, except for the number of people, she'd been raised in a house almost exactly like this one.

"It can be a little overwhelming," Evan murmured just behind her.

Bless his heart. She turned and gave him a crooked smile. "My father was a company vice president before he died. I went to private schools and SMU in Dallas. That's why I settled in Texas, I think. This could have been my home—if you took out all the people and all the personality."

Evan blinked.

"I know." She shrugged. "You thought I was a poor girl from the wrong side of the tracks." Then she sidled close to him and whispered, "If it'll make you feel any better, that's one of my favorite games. Wanna play?"

"Maybe."

She'd been teasing, but he didn't laugh.

"What do I get if I win?" he asked.

At the look in his eyes, Tess's mouth went dry. Okay. They were going to have to resolve the Whitney issue *real* soon.

"Mom's home!" Quatro called just in time, and everybody headed toward the kitchen.

An attractive blond woman was staring into the refrigerator. "I should cook a roast chicken with salad and fruit and some other low-carb veggie. But after a day at the spa, I am just thinking pizza."

"I'm on it," Quatro said.

"Make one a veggie pizza," his mother said.

Quatro grinned. "Does spinach alfredo count?"

She grinned back. "Oh, why not?" Closing the fridge, she advanced toward Tess. "I'm Linda, Woody—sorry—Quatro's mom and Evan's aunt. You must be Tess."

Tess nodded and shook her hand.

"This is nice," Linda said. "We hardly ever meet one of Henry's recipients."

So everybody knew everything in this family. Something she should remember. "Did Evan and Quatro tell you I've been trying to give the money back?"

She nodded. "You're a better woman than I am."

Tess doubted that.

Linda shrugged her shoulders. "I had a massage today and my neck doesn't hurt for the first time in ages. Why don't you book a massage, Evan?"

"And I know just the place." Suggestiveness laced Quatro's voice.

"I hope you're referring to the new sports training facility wing that opened in our spa, and not some sleazy place near the Drag."

"Why, yes, Mother." He gestured for Evan to talk with him later.

Linda rolled her eyes. "You could come with us tomorrow, Evan. Tess, you're welcome, too."

Evan explained, "During vacation, the men all go fishing with Henry and the women head for the spa. Was Mom there?"

"Yes." Linda reached into the fridge again and held up a diet and a regular Coke.

Tess took the diet.

"She and your dad leave day after tomorrow for their cruise," Linda continued, then shot a piercing look at Evan. "They're worried about you. I told them I'd make sure you took time off."

Man. Tess had pegged her as a vapid socialite, but not after that look. That was the kind of look that made a girl stand up straight and quit slouching, which Tess promptly did.

Linda waved Tess to a stool around the kitchen island. "I'm the designated adult this week. But next week, look out."

"Everyone needs to stop obsessing about my life," Evan protested as he slid onto a stool next to Tess. "I'm fine."

"Sure you are," said his aunt.

"I'm working on Evan," Tess blurted out to her surprise.

Linda subjected her to an assessing look as she sipped some bottled water.

Tess had seen that look before. "Are you a lawyer?"

"Does it show?"

"Yeah."

Linda nodded. "Clearly, I need another massage to work out the lawyer kinks. What a pity, right?"

Tess laughed with her.

"Yes, I'm one of Bartholomew's Best corporate lawyers. So's my husband. We don't know what Quatro is going to be yet. Now Jos—she gets off today in about thirty minutes—is thinking finance. If Quatro pursues Internet marketing, then Jos will go international finance. She'll have to make up her mind soon since she'll be a junior next year." She swallowed, then waved her hand. "I'm sorry, I'm assuming you know all about us."

"I know a lot," Tess said.

"We're definitely a family business," Linda said as Quatro hung up the kitchen phone.

While they waited for the pizza to be delivered, they fell into a comfortable pattern of small talk which Tess contrasted with the conversations of her childhood. Actually, those had been more like grillings than conversations, with only child Tess reporting her day's accomplishments—and there had better have been some—and what homework she had yet to complete. She was taught to work hard so she could achieve success, but these people were clearly successful and high achievers and so...relaxed about it. She couldn't miss the undercurrent of affection that ran through their exchanges and while Tess never doubted she was loved, she wondered if she was liked by her parents.

Which brought up Evan. Why was he such a stress bunny?

The doorbell rang. "Evan, I left my purse on the foyer table," his aunt said. "Will you get the money to pay the pizza guy?"

"It'll be my treat." And he left.

Linda watched him, and Tess knew she was still worried.

"I made him turn off his cell phone," Tess told her.

"He'll just turn it back on." Linda turned to her. "Quatro told me you were going to stay in Austin for a while. I want you to understand that you are under no obligation to us. Uncle Henry's gift is just that— a gift. It's yours to do with as you wish."

"Except to give it back."

"Why would you want to? Are you afraid of it?"

"Not exactly afraid—I just don't want to deal with it."

Linda sipped her water. "When faced with a way to accomplish their dreams, some people panic. It's easier for them to have a dream than go about making it come true."

Tess didn't have any secret dreams. "That's not the case here. Henry wanted me to record a CD. My singing is not professional quality."

"She's really bad," Quatro said. "No offense."

"None taken."

But Linda was still studying her.

"I realize you don't know me, but—"

"Oh, I know all about you. Henry always investigates potential recipients."

Tess gave her a shocked look.

"I should say I know your background but not you," Linda amended. "But after Quatro told me about your father, I think I understand more than the facts."

Tess turned to Quatro. "Do you tell your mother *everything*?"

He looked aggrieved. "I don't have anything to do but talk on the cell phone while I'm waiting in the car. I called to let her know we were going to come by and make the CD and, well, she asks these questions and I just—" he made a rolling motion with his hands "—blurt it all out."

Linda laughed.

Tess gave her a thumbs-up. "Well done."

Footsteps sounded in the hallway. Linda leaned forward. "Anything you can do for Evan, thanks. We don't know why he pushes himself the way he does. And it's not healthy. I think you are uniquely qualified to understand that."

Tess nodded just as a pizza box–laden Evan came into the kitchen.

They'd all picked out a slice of pizza when a loud groan announced the arrival of Jocelyn, Quatro's sister.

"I'm dying—or at least my feet are!" She limped into the kitchen and kicked off her pumps.

"This is Tess," Evan said.

"You're Henry's latest. Cool." Jos smiled at her as

she dug in the freezer. Seconds later, she dropped a bag of frozen peas on one foot and a bag of frozen corn on the other. "Ahhh," she sighed.

Tess knew she was working as a waitress. Getting up from the kitchen island, she bent down and picked up one of the discarded shoes to check it out. "No wonder your feet hurt. What do you think you're doing wearing these shoes?"

"Aren't you a waitress, too?" Jos asked, and at this point Tess wasn't surprised that she knew.

"Yes."

"So what's with those boots?"

Tess unzipped one and took it off. "Try it on."

"I don't think we're the same size."

"Doesn't matter."

Jos tugged the boot on and her mouth dropped open. "It's like walking on a pillow!"

"Duh," Tess said to her. "I'll take you shopping for shoes. I know a place here in Austin."

"Would you? Thanks." Jos limped over to the island and inhaled a piece of pizza. "I am so pooped. Wait until next year," she said to her brother. "You'll never last."

Tess had learned that all Bartholomew children followed a certain career path that involved lots of service-industry labor. The interesting thing was that they didn't object.

"So you went through all this?" she asked Evan and he nodded.

He'd been awfully quiet, but she'd been aware of his gaze nearly the whole time. She hoped his aunt hadn't noticed, but had a feeling nothing much escaped the woman.

Tess had a great time. But it seemed the more she laughed and the more she relaxed, the more brooding Evan became. What was his problem?

After they'd finished the pizzas, she trooped upstairs with Quatro and sang into his computer. It was both horrible and wonderful at the same time. And it was funny to watch Linda and Jos attempt to school their expressions until Tess assured them that she had no illusions about how her singing affected others.

The fact that Henry was tone-deaf was apparently not common knowledge, and everyone else had to sing to figure out if they were as well.

It turned out to be one of the best nights of Tess's life, which surprised her a lot. She'd considered herself a loner, and this bunch was unreal. At one point, she asked both Jos and Quatro why they hadn't rebelled and they told her how being a Bartholomew's Best intern was one of the most coveted entry-level jobs in Austin. If they didn't want to do it, nobody was going to make them. No, Jos didn't like being a waitress, but she knew it was part of her education.

They were so well-adjusted, it was weird.

So when Quatro drove her and a silent Evan back to Evan's place, she asked him if he ever felt like rebelling.

He gazed at her for a long moment and said, "I did."

He left her standing with her mouth open as he unlocked the door to his house. Evan a rebel? Who knew.

"And?" she asked.

"And they took me back." He scowled. "I'm tired.

Everything you need should be upstairs, so I'll just say good-night."

"Wait a minute—tell me more about this rebellion. What happened?"

He gazed at her for a long minute. "I was stupid and now I'm not, and I don't plan to be stupid ever again."

"Depends on your definition of stupid, I suppose."

He'd been looking at her mouth as she spoke. Now he raised his eyes to hers. "I got caught in the dot-com crash. Henry and the family bailed me out. I need to pay them back. No time for vacations. End of story."

His voice was deep and the lighting was low. "It doesn't sound as though they hold grudges," Tess said.

She took a step toward him before she realized that it probably wasn't wise.

Up to this point, she'd noticed Evan's potential and that he was a good-looking male. But standing in the shadows in his house at the foot of the stairs, he'd made the transition to good-looking, desirable, prime, hunky *man*.

Tess felt desire tickle all those places only a man could itch.

He wanted to kiss her and she sure wanted to be kissed, but he was waiting for her to make the first move. If she stepped onto the stairs toward the frilly teen-girl guest room, the moment would pass. If she stepped toward his bedroom, there would be a lot more moments.

Unfortunately, now was not the time for hot, serious moments. Not even warm, flirty moments.

Tess deliberately placed a booted foot on the lowest stair. "Good night," she said.

He didn't move, but neither did she. Maybe a friendly moment. Just one, friendly little—

"Go." His voice was a rasp.

Don't you want to kiss me good-night, she started to ask, but the look on his face made her think better of it.

He did want to kiss her good-night, but he wasn't happy about it and frankly, when a man kissed her, Tess wanted him fully behind the kiss.

So she walked up the stairs.

TESS. OH, GREAT. The first thing Evan thought of when he awoke had been his last thought when he went to sleep. He was surprised that he'd slept at all.

Something to distract him from work? Oh, his family would be thrilled to know that he hadn't given Bartholomew's Best a thought in hours.

He carried a horrible secret deep inside: he didn't believe in the Bartholomew's Best creed anymore. It wasn't that he thought it was wrong; it was that he didn't believe it had the same relevance in today's commercial marketplace. He'd analyzed target market surveys, studied data from focus groups and just plain watched people not buying as much as they used to. They weren't investing for long-term, even though they'd end up paying far more in repairs, lost time and replacement. They didn't want to pay for the best—they were just interested in good enough for now.

They were wrong and Uncle Henry's vision was right, which made it impossible to argue against him. Therefore, Evan had to ease in some changes without appearing to compromise the values that had been a part of the family for over a hundred and twenty years.

He could see what was going to happen to the company and so would Jos and Quatro when they had more education and experience. The store would struggle, profits would fall and ultimately, some gigantic monolith would buy Bartholomew's Best because of its reputation. They'd keep the name and trash the culture.

Evan had ideas and was working within a narrow window of time. Like now, because right after the summer break, it was time to gear up for the make-it-or-break-it Christmas season, and then he'd have to start over again next spring.

But, unless Henry relented, that was his current situation. And since he couldn't think about the store, that meant he was thinking about Tess, a person he hadn't even known existed yesterday morning.

Evan looked at the clock, not surprised that he'd awakened at his regular time, even though he'd turned off the alarm.

He wondered if Tess was awake. Normally, he'd head upstairs to the exercise equipment, but he didn't want to wake her up.

So his mind wandered and it wandered into areas like what Tess looked like sleeping, what she slept in and where she would have been sleeping if he'd kissed her last night the way he'd wanted to.

And his family thought this was relaxing?

He should have taken his parents up on their offer to cruise with them, but there was something pathetic about a twenty-eight-year-old man on a cruise with his parents unless it was a family celebration or they needed his help. But his parents were totally independent and the only thing they were celebrating was each other, which he was *not* going to think about.

Evan got up and pulled on a pair of workout shorts and a T-shirt and went to check for any messages on his phones.

There was nothing on either his cell or his land line.

"Okay, now what am I supposed to do?" he asked aloud.

"You make coffee like a normal person," said a grumpy voice from the stairs. "Then you eat breakfast."

A yawning Tess fingercombed her hair off her face and padded barefoot past him. She wore a gray T-shirt that ended about mid-thigh and probably not a whole lot else, judging by the movement beneath the shirt.

Longing tore through him and it didn't matter that Tess had no doubt calculated her appearance to have just that effect. It worked, that was the point. Worked very well. So well that he wanted to sling her over his shoulder and haul her off to his bed. Once there, *he'd* get her singing in tune.

But he didn't do that. The thing was, Tess was temporary and the Bartholomew family was all about long-term. The philosophy rubbed off on a guy.

Tess was now in his kitchen, looking in his cabinets which required that she raise her arm, which resulted in the corresponding rise of the hemline of her nightshirt that matched the rise in his libido.

She had great legs and he hadn't considered himself a leg man before. He hadn't considered himself a Tess type before, either. She was so clearly one of those women a man could lose himself with and then always remember after she moved on. Because she would move on.

She pulled down an ancient jar of instant coffee and made a face at him. "You're kidding?"

"I pick up breakfast in the downstairs coffee shop on the way to work."

Tess set the jar on the counter none too gently and opened the fridge. "Hello-o-o-o," she mimicked an echo. "You don't even have orange juice. I didn't expect milk, but at least OJ makes a good mixer."

She bent down to open the lower drawers and Evan sighed as her T-shirt inevitably rode up.

At the sound, she turned her head without straightening. "What?"

"You have great legs." Maybe he could tweak his anti-fling philosophy a bit.

"Thanks." She went back to looking in the fridge.

"That was not news to you."

She stood and shut the door. "No." Smiling, she came to the kitchen bar and propped her elbows on the granite surface. "This is a fabulous kitchen and you don't cook."

"Why bother when it's only me?"

"It's relaxing. It's nutritious and it involves the senses."

"Do you cook?"

"I used to." She straightened and frowned. "I cooked family dinners. I planned menus and I like to think I was pretty good." She raised an eyebrow at him. "My motivation was that if the meals were really great, then one or both of my parents would come home to eat them with me."

"But they didn't—I know where this story is going. Is it true, or is it another cautionary tale for me?"

Tess's face closed. "It's true."

Which made him feel bad. "I apologize."

"It's not your fault."

"The snarky comment was."

"Yeah, that was pretty bad. You'll have to make it up to me."

Although he'd already apologized, he asked, "How?"

"We should cook this week."

"Week?" The veins in his temples began to throb. "You're staying here a week?"

She stretched. "In Austin, if not *here* here. Maybe longer."

Evan couldn't see the hemline from this angle, but he could definitely see the T-shirt material stretch and move over her breasts. "Stop it."

"Why?" She drew her hands down her sides to her thighs and managed to make that sexy, too. "You like it."

"That's why."

"I like it, too." She came from behind the bar. "I like the way you look at me. It makes me hot knowing that you want to run your hands all over me and that there's nothing between us but this—" she pulled at her sleeve "—flimsy fabric."

She was manipulating him and honestly, he didn't care. In fact, he was glad he could be manipulated. He was all for it.

She'd moved close to him, but when he reached for her, she sidestepped him.

"Not until you resolve the Whitney issue."

The words *Whitney* and *issue* puckered her mouth. "You're kidding."

"No. When I said you needed lots of sex, I didn't necessarily mean with me."

"Then what was all this about?"

She drew her finger down his beard-roughened jaw. "Motivation." Her hip brushed against his as she walked by.

There was a buzzing in his head and his fingertips tingled. And the condition of his groin went without saying as he watched her and that great walk of hers. "Are you always so direct?"

"Only when the situation calls for it."

He stared at her. Actually, he was staring at her thigh, which was revealed by the way she propped one foot on the stairs. "And this situation did?"

"Oh, yes. You definitely needed shaking up."

He was shaken all right. "Good job."

She grinned. "Get ready and let's hit the grocery store."

He'd thought she was going to say *hit the sheets*. When Tess started up the stairs, it was all Evan could do to keep from following her. "Tess, where is this going?" he called.

"I told you—to the grocery store. On the way, you can tell me your favorite foods."

"You know what I mean."

She bowed her head for a moment. "Does it have to go anywhere? Can't it just be?"

He watched as she continued up the stairs. *Just be.* That's what Henry had said.

He sure hoped Uncle Henry's state of being and Tess's were different.

5

"I SWEAR, THIS IS like giving a Martian a tour of Earth."

Tess dragged Evan away from the little bundles of fresh herbs. She'd recently nudged him away from the lettuce. Maybe he had a thing for greenery. She made a mental note to buy some plants for his house.

"When was the last time you went grocery shopping?" she asked him.

"I don't. At least not in a huge place like this."

They were in one of the grocery chain's flagship stores, so it was one of the bigger ones. Tess noticed that Evan was looking at the people as much as the produce.

"You know, my uncle and the board of directors—"

"And I'll bet you're related to every one."

"By blood or marriage," he acknowledged. "They're all about being aware of average people and cultural trends and not being out of touch. And I thought I was pretty much in tune. I mean, I'm the guy who runs the surveys. But this—" he waved his arm "—is so basic and so much a part of people's lives and I'm just blown away by the variety and the weird packaging. That tells me my outlook is skewed."

"I gotta tell you, a lot of people don't cook, either. But the stores have compensated. I'll show you all the prepackaged stuff there is out there. And we're going to start by cheating, too. Check out the salads in a bag." Tess showed him.

"Hey, here's that stuff that always costs so much in restaurants." He held a bag of mixed baby greens.

"But you get more here. Toss it in the basket. Now, about veggies. Broccoli—thumbs-up, thumbs-down?"

"Thumbs-up, I guess. It comes with enough entrées."

"Okay. Get a bunch and put it in the sack. Next up, eggplant." She showed him the purple oblong vegetable. Actually, she was hoping he wasn't a secret eggplant lover because, well, though the purple was attractive and the shape was sensuous, frankly, it reminded her of a long-ago moussaka disaster.

"I have absolutely no idea," he said.

She put it back. "Artichoke?"

"I—"

Tess grabbed two. "They're fun to eat."

She had a few menus planned and discovered that he had an aversion to pasta, which, frankly crimped her style. "I thought everybody liked spaghetti," she'd said when he told her.

"Not everybody worked in an Italian restaurant."

"Even with alfredo sauce?" Not that she had any business eating such rich food.

"If I'm forced."

Now, he shook his head as he gazed around the produce department. "There must be forty-five kinds of apples."

"When was the last time you ate an apple?"

He looked startled. "I don't know."

Tess gathered a sampling. "This week is going to be good for you. More sleep, better food. You'll feel great."

She didn't know when or why she'd decided on the week time frame, but now it was stuck in her head. "When you go back to work, promise me you'll brown-bag it a couple of days a week so you get some fresh stuff in you."

They passed out of produce and headed toward dairy, which, inexplicably, was next to the wine department.

"Check out these prices." While she'd been getting low-fat milk, he'd detoured into the wine department. "I'd forgotten about restaurant price markups."

Even after working in a bar, Tess didn't know a whole lot about more expensive wines, since they didn't stock them. "Why don't you choose a couple of bottles?"

By the time she'd picked up orange juice, he'd put three in the cart.

After selecting breakfast stuff, meats and the basics to stock his kitchen, they went back to his house to fix breakfast, or, since it was getting late, brunch.

She made Evan help cook, if cracking eggs and scrambling them with a fork could be called cooking.

But it was a start, and it was fun. She also let him

cook bacon, which he burned. That was okay, because Tess wasn't a huge bacon fan and she tended to burn it herself—which was why she had microwave sausage links for backup.

They had to stick bread under the broiler for toast since Evan didn't have a toaster.

"I'll pick one up at the store," he said.

"I thought you weren't allowed in the store."

"I'm not allowed in the corporate offices."

Tess thought about her one trip to Bartholomew's Best and remembered the sticker shock. "Hey, what kind of employee discount do you get?"

"Fifteen percent, same as everybody else."

"Doesn't sound like much."

"Our markup isn't as large as a regular department store."

"Why not?"

Evan exhaled. "Trying to stay competitive with prices."

Tess didn't comment. They'd stuffed themselves with the sort of breakfast fed to farmhands after two hours of chores. Tess felt pleasantly sluggish and not inclined to start on the dishes.

"So what exactly is it that you do for the store?" she asked.

"I analyze sales data and trends."

"Sounds fascinating." Not.

"I also work with a marketing research firm."

"Not those people who call you during dinner with questionnaires that take forty-five minutes to answer?"

"Um, probably." He gave her a sheepish look as he rubbed at his unshaven face.

Hmm. Tess sipped at her coffee and studied him. He was looking better after the night's sleep—attractive, even though he was *way* overdressed in khakis and a golf shirt. And yet he hadn't shaved.

"You're staring."

"I'm evaluating." Tess put down her mug. "I like the preppy-gone-bad look you've got going, but I'm thinking jeans and a torn T-shirt might be even better."

He gazed at her warily. "I don't have a torn T-shirt."

"We can fix that."

"And why would we want to?"

"For when you go see Whitney." Making sure Evan was a free man had become Tess's number one priority.

She had absolutely no doubt he was already a free man, but she knew he needed closure. And she kind of wanted Whitney to have second thoughts. It would be good for his ego.

"Whitney isn't a torn T-shirt kind of woman."

"Every woman is a torn T-shirt kind of gal. Come on. Let's see what's in your closet."

"The dishes…"

"Will be here when we finish." She eyed him as they passed the living room windows. "Another two days and your beard will be perfect."

"Whitney doesn't like beards, either."

Good, Tess thought, because she didn't like Whitney.

"I don't know." Evan had stopped at the hall mirror and was rubbing his face.

The light from the foyer hit him in a particularly attractive way, not to mention highlighting some interesting muscles in his back.

Well, there was that exercise equipment in the spare room upstairs. And now that she checked out the view from behind, she decided that he wore his pants too loose.

Tess suddenly wanted him in a pair of jeans. And then out of the jeans, but all in good—or bad—time.

Okay. He was just going to have to face Whitney with the beard he had. "Call her."

"Pardon?"

"Call Whitney." Tess pointed to the phone on the hall table. "Call her now."

Evan's eyes met hers in the mirror and he reached for the phone. "And then what?"

"Ask her for coffee or lunch or something."

"And the reason I'm asking?"

"You have to have a reason? Shouldn't she want to see you?"

He stared down at the phone receiver in his hand. "Do I have to see her at all?"

Men. "You can't just blurt it out on the phone. You two have history. You'll have to break it off in person."

"When did 'resolve the issue' become break it off?"

He had to be kidding. "After the way you looked at me a few hours ago? Puhleeze."

"You—you're very self-assured."

And he was stalling. "Because you're a slam dunk, honey."

What he needed was a little motivation. Tess gave

him her sultriest look and sauntered over, noting that Evan watched her intently, so intently that he allowed her all the way into his personal space before he even thought about backing up. She could tell the instant it occurred to him to do so. Too late. She took hold of the collar of his preppy little shirt and pulled him toward her, standing on her toes until her mouth was next to his.

She waited until she felt his hands slowly move around her waist and urge her toward him. He tried to close the millimeter between their mouths but Tess insinuated a finger next to his lips. "So do you feel like making up—or breaking up?"

"I feel like kissing you."

"Not until you're a free man." She released his lapels and stepped out of his arms. "Now call Whitney."

As it turned out, Evan hunched his back to her, clearly wanting privacy, so Tess rolled her eyes and returned to the kitchen to start on the dishes.

She had just discovered that a sample dishwasher detergent packet was still taped inside the door when Evan came into the room.

"You've never used your dishwasher?"

"I'd run out of glasses before I had a full load. I just wash them by hand."

"Not today." Tess removed the instructions and the detergent sample.

"So when is the showdown?" she asked when Evan didn't tell her.

"Whitney's job is keeping her very busy."

"So lunch is out?"

"Very out. Today, tomorrow, and Friday."

"Did you try dinner?"

"She has a tai chi class tonight, a late meeting tomorrow and her parents are arriving Friday to spend the weekend."

"Hmm." Tess wasn't sure she bought the parental visit, but that was a great excuse. She should remember it. "And coffee?"

Evan had methodically cleared the table and scraped the dishes, all without meeting her eyes. "Uh, she's pretty booked."

Tess touched his arm. "Are you saying that she couldn't manage to fit you in for so much as coffee for the next five days? Tell me you didn't ask about next week."

"I—"

"Evan, you are sounding like a complete wimp. I have to say that it's very unattractive."

He exhaled. "It's payback. When we first started going out I…may have canceled on her more than I should. It was just after I'd come back to the store and I wanted to do a good job."

"Oh, she needs to get over herself. So, she let you dangle—you let yourself dangle—for two years while she was in…London, was it?"

"Well…it was easier."

"Easier than what?."

"I didn't know if our problems were because of distance or incompatibility. We got along fine on our visits, except after last Christmas…and I knew she was moving back in February and frankly, I was busy and it wasn't the time to have one of those talks."

"Okay, the icky wimpiness factor is canceled out by your honorability, I guess we'll call it. You remained committed to the relationship. Very good. But now, you're at ground zero and it's time to reclaim your manhood."

"I'm going to like that." He gave her a look.

Tess couldn't believe he'd just told her he hadn't bothered to officially end his relationship and he was giving her a look like that.

She kind of liked it. "Not that way. You're going to confront Whitney and give her an ultimatum. Go put on a casual hot outfit." Tess shooed him out of the kitchen.

"Casual hot? You mean shorts?"

"You do have great legs, but no, I meant—" She saw his grin. "You're lucky I don't brain you with a wooden spoon."

Still grinning, he headed for his room.

Honestly. She was absolutely furious with the unknown Whitney. Evan was a nice guy, in the best sense. If Whitney didn't want him, she should throw him back into the pond.

There was always the chance that confronted with Evan— She interrupted her thoughts to shout "Hey! Don't shave!"

Anyway, there was always the chance that Whitney would want him back.

Soooo. Maybe Tess should refresh Evan's memory on why that would be a bad idea.

He returned just as she'd loaded the last of the dishes.

Tess groaned.

"What?" He gestured down at himself.

He wore a navy blazer, khaki slacks and an open-necked white shirt.

"*That's* your idea of casual hot?"

"No tie! And look—no socks!" He pulled up his pants leg.

"Oh, you're quite the rebel." Actually, under some other circumstances, the look might work. Tess squinted. Maybe with a T-shirt and jeans. "You need more beard."

"So you've said."

"Let's go see what's in your closet." Tess led the way to his bedroom. "We'll also have to practice your scowling and your frankly-my-dear look."

"Maybe I should write her a note and send flowers," he grumbled.

But Tess wanted Whitney to understand exactly what she'd lost so she would never be piggy with good available men again. Whitney had violated one of the unwritten codes of the sisterhood—basically, if you don't want him, let someone else have him.

Tess smiled to herself as she entered the bedroom. She would be the rebound relationship. That suited her just fine. Short and intense—excellent rebound material.

Feeling cheerful about the upcoming week, she opened Evan's closet, flipped on the light...and shrieked.

"What?"

"You have got to be an alien, because I know you're not gay."

"Excuse me?"

"Your closet—the suits—lots and lots of suits—are here, the shirts are there, lined up by color, all on wooden hangers...obsessive-compulsive?"

"You have a thing against neatness?" he countered.

"There's neat and there's..." She waved at his closet.

"I like it. A bunch of us were talking about those makeover shows on cable and I watched a few of them. I hired a closet-organizing company."

He would. Tess was relieved. "I guess that's okay. However, what's in here is not. Where are your jeans?"

Evan stepped around her and pulled out a pair neatly folded on a wooden hangar. They were dark blue and creased. Tess fingered them. And starched.

She shook her head and pulled them off the hangar. "You don't treat jeans this way. You have to rumple them." She crumpled them up and dropped them onto the floor where she proceeded to stomp on them, to Evan's amusement.

"Okay, now try them." She held them out.

He tossed them over his shoulder and waited.

"Go ahead." She gestured.

His eyes never leaving hers, he slowly slid the end of his leather belt through the loop of the pants he was wearing.

"Oh." She turned around and sat on the bed. Best

not to start something they couldn't finish. Yet. "I'll be over here."

"Why, Tess." He laughed softly, sending a shiver up her spine. "This is a side of you I haven't seen before."

"What do you mean?"

A snap popped. "Modesty."

Yeah, right. "This isn't modesty so much as a time-and-place issue."

"I've got time. And this is the place." There was the unmistakable sound of a zipper unzipping.

She laughed. "You're just desperate for me to turn around and see what you've got."

"Just desperate."

"Hmm. Good. It'll give you an edge."

She heard him remove his pants and debated a quick underwear check, but didn't.

"Last chance," he called softly.

She could turn around, except they both knew that if she did, more clothes would come off before Evan got around to putting on those jeans. Well, so what? Whitney was toast, anyway.

She could hear him breathing. She could hear *herself* breathing. The fizz of anticipation ran through her veins, but…but there were rules in situations like this and she was not one of those women who ignored the rules. "You'd lose your edge," she said on a sigh.

"And I am looking forward to that."

She laughed at the sincerity in his voice.

Okay, so here she was, sitting on the bed in an attractive man's bedroom and he was taking off his pants.

And what was she doing? Dressing him to go to another woman.

And about that—he'd better plan on taking Tess with him because she wanted to see this Whitney person. She wasn't interested in a formal introduction, but a woman who could hold on to Evan when she wasn't even on the same continent—and hold on to him for two years—was a woman Tess wanted to check out.

She heard him pull on his jeans and was suddenly restless. She bounced. Bounced again. Harder—just testing in advance. The bed was a little firm for her taste, but at least there weren't any squeaky springs.

She heard Evan inhale and then the sound of a snap and zipper.

"These are kind of tight."

She turned around and had immediate second thoughts. Whitney must not see him in jeans. Ever. "Mmm. Yes, they are." Her quick aging had done nothing more than leave dusty marks on them, yet he still looked good. "Turn around."

"So you can check out my butt?"

"Of course."

Evan laughed and turned around.

"Evan, Evan, Evan. That butt deserves a better pair of jeans."

"These are designer jeans!"

"And when a designer-jeans occasion comes up, you're covered." She got off the bed and entered his closet. "I'm not seeing any T-shirts."

He slid open a drawer and showed her a row of

white folded undershirts. And boxer briefs, for the record. Extremely acceptable.

"Uh, that's for advanced bad boys." An image of a scowling Evan in jeans and white T-shirt slouched against a motorcycle slid into her mind. He looked good next to the motorcycle. Maybe she should buy a motorcycle instead of a car. After all, here was the perfect accessory scowling right next to her.

"Oh, that's the expression!" She dragged him in front of the dresser mirror. "See how your mouth manages to kind of twist itself so it's frowning and smiling at the same time? That's a great sneering scowl." She patted his shoulder. "You're very talented. Scowls like that just can't be taught."

"Tess…"

"And you've got the voice to go with it!" She rubbed her shoulders. "I'm getting shivers. Look." She held out her arm and showed him the goose bumps.

"Whitney does not respond to this."

"Newsflash, Evan. She's not responding to Mr. Preppy, either."

He stepped into his shoes. "I can't figure you out, Tess. Are you for Whitney or against her?"

It depended on Whitney's worthiness, but Tess wasn't going to tell him that. "I'm *for* you. Now come on. We're going shopping for jeans. And if we don't find any, we're going to run over these with the car in your driveway until they look better. By the way, I can't believe you drive a Honda sedan and don't quote me any more statistics."

EVAN STARED AT HIMSELF in the dressing-room mirror and hitched the latest pair of jeans up higher. Of course, Tess would tug them down. And then she would complain that they didn't fit—as though it was his fault—and he'd be sent back to the dressing room to model another pair.

So he beat her to it and changed to the smaller size, imagining Whitney's wrinkled nose when she saw the molded fit.

He used to think her nose was cute when she did the wrinkling thing and he told her so. Apparently *cute* was now a derogatory term. Whitney broke herself of her nose-wrinkling habit, but Evan could tell she still wanted to whenever she saw something distasteful because her nostrils flared with the effort of not wrinkling. It wasn't cute, but he had to admit it had more effect.

He didn't tell her that.

Tess was much more demonstrative when she found something to her distaste—say, ill-fitting jeans. She wrinkled her whole face, closed her eyes and made gagging sounds as she gave whatever he was wearing a thumbs-down.

But when he had on a pair with potential, well. She sat back in the chair, her eyelids lowered, and her lips curved in a dreamy half smile that told him she was thinking of sex, maybe even sex with him. Talk about positive reinforcement. He'd tried on dozens of jeans hoping for that smile.

Evan had never seen Whitney's mouth in a dreamy half smile. Sexy, yes. Whitney could be that, but sensuous, no. In fact, until meeting Tess, he hadn't appreciated the difference.

Could two women be more different, yet equally confusing?

Evan had Whitney pretty much figured out: there had once been a spark between them. Though it had long since died out, each of them felt they could re-kindle it—when they had the time.

By unspoken mutual agreement, they'd put their relationship in suspended animation while they concentrated on their careers. Whitney was in international finance law, and no Bartholomew had that expertise.

Evan admitted her profession had been part of her appeal. She'd be a great addition to the Bartholomew team and she understood, or he'd thought she understood, working long hours.

Pointing to a sacrificed relationship would enhance Whitney's reputation with her company.

Uncle Henry would just think Evan had been stupid.

Actually, he'd been able to wave his relationship around as proof that he wasn't working too much. His association with Whitney had been extremely low-maintenance, and there hadn't been any reason to end it until he'd met Tess.

Tess. Now Tess, he couldn't figure out.

She'd been very up front about what she wanted—but had she really?

He hadn't kissed her. He'd hardly touched her. He hadn't seen her naked.

All he had were promises—or did he?

When I said you needed lots of sex, I didn't necessarily mean with me.

Tease or truth?

So, with Tess, all he really had were a couple of suggestive looks, a flash of leg and a few smart remarks.

And somebody who bullied him into trying on five thousand pairs of jeans.

"Evan, if you don't get out here, I'm coming in!"

Fun and games in the dressing room. He could go for that. He stayed put and a few minutes later, Tess knocked on the shuttered swing doors.

"Yes?" Evan tried to remember if anyone else was in the dressing room.

"Are you decent?"

"Does it matter?"

"Nope."

Evan slid the lock bar and pulled open the door. "I figured as much."

Tess gave him the once-over and stepped inside the dressing room.

"And we have a winner." She smiled, a dreamy half smile.

His mouth grew dry, but he didn't reach for her. Not this time. This time, he wanted her to reach for *him*.

But Tess being Tess, she didn't, which left him irritated and frustrated. "They're too tight. One washing and I'll never get them on again."

"They're prewashed."

"They're still too tight. You can see—" Pretty much all the jewels in the family vault, he'd been going to say, when behind him Tess tugged at his waistband to check the fit and then skimmed her hands across his backside. His pulse pounded. He drew his fingers into a fist.

"Feels like a good fit to me." Her hands lingered and patted and pulled, skimmed his thighs, and generally caused complete havoc with his nervous system.

Inevitably, Evan grew hard, and because of these jeans and Tess's view of the mirror, she knew it. If she didn't move *immediately*, he was going to turn around and—

"Seems like they have just enough give in them." And with a final pat, she left the dressing room.

The woman made him crazy. He should have grabbed her when he had the chance.

Evan stood there, breathing deeply and wondering if she expected him to try on more jeans, or if these were the golden pair. He squatted in them and nearly cut himself in two. If she made him buy this style, he was also getting the pair in the next size up.

Something black came flying over the top of the door. "Try this on with those jeans."

"What makes you think I've still got them on?" he grumbled at her.

"Why would you ever take them off? They're perfect for you."

Okay, maybe he wouldn't buy the ones in the larger size.

6

WITH THE MEMORY of Tess's smile and the sound of her husky voice foremost in his brain, Evan figured he'd wear his new jeans and the T-shirt with the bizarre phrase that was so cool he didn't get it at all, out of the store and head directly over to Whitney's office.

But no. Apparently Tess was supposed to go shopping with Jos at four o'clock.

"But—" *What am I supposed to do?* That's what he'd been about to say and it sounded pitiful. He'd managed to occupy himself without Tess for twenty-eight years, so an evening alone shouldn't be too difficult.

Since Tess hadn't bought a new car, Jos was picking her up. As she sat on the steps in the foyer and waited, Evan paced around her even though he tried not to.

"Are you worried about Whitney?" she asked.

"No."

"Then you're suffering from work withdrawal."

"Hardly." He was suffering from Tess lust. Really not good when he analyzed it, so he avoided thinking a whole lot.

"It would be normal. Your routine has been upset

and you have nothing to take its place," she continued, maybe oblivious, maybe not. "What are you going to do while I'm gone?"

"I don't know."

"I knew it." She stood. "Come with me. I have an assignment for you."

He followed her into the kitchen and she got out a box of brownie mix.

"You can make brownies while I'm gone. Jos has to be at the restaurant by six, so this is a quickie trip. You and I can cook the rest of dinner after I get back."

"Brownies?" She expected him to make brownies?

"Evan." She flipped the box around. "Simple directions. The mix even comes with its own baking pan." She opened the box and shook out the pan and the mix. "See?"

He saw. He also heard a car horn. Tess waggled her fingers. "Buh-bye!"

Was it just yesterday he'd eaten brownies? Evan recalled the taste exploding in his mouth. Actually, he'd only had a piece of brownie. He deserved a whole brownie.

Did Tess like brownies? She must, or she wouldn't have bought the mix.

Evan stared at the box. He could do this.

It turned out to be insultingly easy. Give a man a brownie and he ate for a day. Teach him how to bake and he wasn't going to fit into tight jeans.

As the aroma of baking brownies permeated his home, Evan, for the first time in a surprising number of hours, thought about Bartholomew's Best. He wasn't supposed to be thinking about the store, and he tried not to, but the more he tried, the more he failed.

There were still no messages on his phones. With his computer locked in his office, he missed his e-mail. It was possible to find an Internet café and access his account, but he'd rather have his laptop. He could use this time off to organize some files, review notes, that kind of thing.

That kind of thing was cheating, which was why security had locked his laptop in his office.

But what about personal e-mail? He might be missing something important.

Feeling restless, Evan wandered back into the kitchen. Maybe there was something he could do to prepare for dinner. Tess had said something about steak.

Evan set the table. It took about two minutes.

And then he got a brilliant idea. *Oprah.* He would watch *Oprah. Oprah* appeared in all Bartholomew's Best sales demographics and he had watched tapes before. Her show came on in the late afternoon, about now. He could watch her live—or less taped than usual.

Evan turned on the TV and found *Oprah* in progress. This was good. He took a notebook from the kitchen desk and prepared to study *Oprah.*

Unfortunately, the rest of *Oprah's* show lasted longer than the twenty minutes that the brownies had left to cook, which Evan forgot—or not exactly forgot, since the aroma was ever present—but he hadn't set the timer. And the chocolate aroma became more of a bitter chocolate smell and then a definite scorched stench. He ran for the oven.

Fortunately, it appeared as though the edges of the paper pan were contributing to most of the smoke. After the brownies cooled slightly, Evan turned them out onto a plate where he proceeded to cut off the burnt edge all the way around.

Then he cut the remaining block into neat squares and arranged them on the plate. There. Tess would never know.

Between *Oprah* and the brownies, he felt very domestic.

Excellent. He was walking the walk of the suburban housewife. He was getting insight he could use and was not wasting time.

"Hi, honey, I'm ho-ome!" The front door closed.

"In the kitchen," he called. They sounded like a sitcom.

"We found Jos a couple of pairs of shoes and the pads to go in them. Now that she knows what she's looking for, she'll be okay. Yum." Tess inhaled. "Look what you did." She flashed him a brilliant smile and he felt irrationally proud.

She took one of his neat squares and gazed at the plate as she chewed. "A little toasted on the edges, huh?"

"How can you tell? They don't taste burnt."

"You cut off the edges. I've done the same thing."

Evan felt a connection. Yes, he and Tess, the most undomestic woman he'd ever met, were having a moment over brownies that he, himself, had baked.

She brushed her fingers together. "We're going to spoil our dinner."

Evan wasn't interested in dinner. He was interested in, oh, her collarbone, revealed by the formfitting tank top she wore. He was interested in the way the neckline gaped a little sometimes. He was interested in the way her skirt hugged her hips and thighs. He was interested in her laugh. He was interested in the habit she had of raking her hair off her face and the way her shirt came up just enough to expose a sliver of toned stomach. And her arms. She had a little definition going on, no doubt from carrying heavy trays of drinks. He was interested in them—the arms.

All that ranked higher than mere dinner, but, since she'd thrust a huge metal grill thing at him, he supposed dinner was going to have to do.

TESS WISHED HE WOULDN'T look at her like that.

Talk about building up a severe case of expectations. Somehow, a teasing *maybe* on her part had become *it's a matter of time and it better be good* on his part.

This wasn't like her, and she suspected it wasn't like Evan, either.

It would help if she hadn't met his family—if she hadn't liked his family. She'd been afraid Jos and Quatro were robot children, but away from the adults in their lives, they were normal, no doubt because of the jobs they'd had.

Those Bartholomews were clever in the way they raised future generations.

But back to the problem at hand, which was Evan.

Tess had meant to keep it light and then move on, but Evan was forgetting the light part.

She was afraid that by taking away Evan's focus, Henry had created a vacuum that Tess had inadvertently filled. She'd become Evan's total focus.

His vacation happiness had become her responsibility and she already felt the weight of it. Evan and his family screamed responsibility, and Tess knew from experience that it wasn't for her.

THE NEXT MORNING, after hours of talking and not so much as a platonic good-night kiss the night before, Evan stood in front of his dresser mirror. "I can't go into Whitney's firm looking like this."

Surprisingly, Tess agreed. "You're right. You can't."

His relief was short-lived.

"Take off your shirt."

As far as he could tell, she didn't have a replacement shirt in mind. Warily, he pulled the black T-shirt over his head.

Tess stared at him and blinked three times in succession. "Oh."

Well, that wasn't a good sound, not from a woman seeing his chest for the first time.

A smile played around her lips. "Hello, muscles," she crooned and traced a finger along one of his ribs. "My name is Tess. *Very* glad to meet you."

"That tickles."

"Tickles good, or tickles bad?"

"Try it with your tongue, and I'll let you know."

She arched an eyebrow. "Getting feisty, are we?"

"I'm way past feisty." He grabbed her wrists and hauled her to him, the shirt bunched between them. "And you know it and if you don't, I'm telling you now."

Her eyes glazed a little. "I know," she whispered.

He bent his head, but Tess gave the tiniest of pushes and he reluctantly released her. "You're driving me insane," he said.

"I know," she repeated. "I'm driving myself insane."

"I can fix that."

"I know," she said a third time.

Why wait? was what he started to say, but she walked out of the room. Carrying his shirt.

He followed her all the way into the kitchen where she rummaged in the telephone desk until she found a pair of scissors.

"What are you doing?"

"Tweaking your confront-the-girlfriend look." She snipped at his sleeve, and then ripped it the rest of the way off. Above the sound of the second sleeve ripping, he asked, "Wouldn't it be easier to just cut it?"

"Then the edges wouldn't be ragged."

"Right."

"Ragged edges draw attention to your arms." She snipped a dangling thread.

Apparently, ragged was good, threads were bad.

"Do I want to draw attention to my arms?"

"Yes."

He felt inordinately pleased and couldn't resist a little flexing. "I thought they were looking too pasty."

"Yes."

He hadn't expected her to agree. He stopped flexing to find her watching him.

"Spray tan," she said.

"No way." She was nuts. "I know what that is. A guy has to wrap his package in a glorified paper jockstrap—"

"Only if you want to."

A small sound escaped his throat. "And then he gets spray-painted."

"Exactly. Have you got a copy of the Yellow Pages handy?"

"Forget it."

She tossed him the shirt. "It'll be the finishing touch."

He tugged on the T-shirt. "But this isn't me."

Tess was digging in the lower cabinet beneath the phone and found the Yellow Pages on her own. "Of course it's you."

"Whitney knows I don't dress like this."

"Evan, it's my opinion that Whitney hasn't really looked at you in quite some time. Our goal is to *make* her look at you."

"Why? Wouldn't it be easier not to stir things up?" At some point, Evan realized he'd decided this was a pro forma meeting to officially end what had ended long ago.

"Because she needs to understand that you and your acceptance of the current state of your relationship have changed. You confront her looking the way you always look and she'll dismiss you the way she did when you phoned her. Confront her looking different and she'll believe you when you tell her you want to take your relationship out of limbo. She'll believe you because you are going to act differently, too." She grinned. "Besides, you're going to be quite the eye candy after we get you tanned."

Eye candy. Cool. He could do eye candy.

Tess spread the thick book open and leaned over it. Today, she had on another one of her tanks, this one a flesh color, and a short, tight denim skirt. For once, she didn't wear the boots, but she had on high-heeled sandals that didn't have any backs. In fact, most of her foot was bare. Her toes were painted a metallic blue.

Evan was quite sure that Whitney's toes had never been blue unless she'd been suffering from lack of oxygen at the time.

Eye candy. "You're sure about the tan?"

"Absolutely." She reached for the phone.

He was not sure about the tan. "Okay, I'll agree to the tan, if you'll do something for me."

"What?" Tess punched in a phone number.

Seeing her with the phone had reminded him of offices and the fact that he couldn't get into his. "I want my laptop. Since I can't get into my office, I want you to get it for me."

"So you can work?"

"Just e-mail and other stuff. I didn't get a chance to shut down properly and let people know I'm on vacation. I promise I won't work." Much.

Tess eyed him as she made an appointment to get him spray-painted.

"Okay." She hung up the phone.

"Was that okay to me or to the tan place?"

"Both. Tuck your shirt in."

He tucked. "Good. Now about your clothes."

She cocked a hip against her fist. "What about them?"

"Don't get me wrong, *I* like them. But you'll need an outfit that blends in with the corporate world more. Do you have anything?"

Her face turned stony. "You mean a skirt down to my calves, a navy blue jacket, a blouse with a floppy bow, and smart-girl glasses?"

"Yeah."

"*No.*"

"Then it looks like we're going shopping again."

She looked outraged. "I am *not* going to dress like that. Break into your office, sure. Play corporate Barbie? Not a chance."

Evan took her arm. "We'll discuss this later."

TESS FOLLOWED a tanned and decidedly hunky Evan down the carpeted corridor. The heel of his new boots left an imprint in the plush carpet and Tess amused herself by trying to match his long stride.

Yes, between the boots, the tan and the clothes, he carried himself differently, and she noticed the looks he got from all the women—*all* the women—they passed.

It had taken a whole lot of talking and a whole lot of promising that she'd go snatch his computer for him to get him to agree to let her tag along. She was only there in case Whitney…well, she supposed she was there in case Whitney wanted him, because why wouldn't she? Evan was very wantable.

So, yes, Tess was there to…to remind Evan that…

Hmm. All this time, she'd assumed that Evan and Whitney would call it quits. Anyone could see that their relationship was already over except for The Talk. But Evan looked so good…and if Whitney *did* want to pick up where they'd left off…Tess had no right to interfere. She didn't consider dressing Evan and prompting this ambush meeting *interfering*. It was preparing, that's what it was.

Anyway, Whitney knew they were on the way up and she wasn't happy about it. Tess was glad Evan hadn't backed down when Whitney had tried to blow him off again. Personally, she attributed it to the jeans or maybe the sleeveless T-shirt. He wasn't sold on the tan, but that's because he couldn't see how it defined the sinewy muscles in his arms.

Tess could. Sigh.

They reached what Tess dubbed the baby lawyer pool and the tiny offices that were more like glorified cubicles with doors to provide clients with the illusion of privacy.

Breathing deeply and easily, Tess glanced around. She hadn't been in an office building in years and was pleased that the closed-in feeling that had assaulted her at the end of her office worker days wasn't present. "I hope the walls are thin so I can eavesdrop easier."

"Tess, please let me introduce you."

"No, no, no. This is between the two of you. If she sees me, then she'll think I'm the reason you're here."

"But you are the reason I'm here."

"But not in the way she'll think."

He gave her a lazy smile, one that looked good with his tan. "No, she'll have the right idea."

Wow. A smile like that had a woman wondering if she could book an emergency leg wax.

Tess plopped down—her knees might have had something to do with that—onto a chair in the make-shift waiting area and gestured for Evan to knock on the door.

He tapped, not as forcefully as Tess would have liked, but at least he was here, making something happen.

"Come in," a feminine voice called. High-pitched feminine. One might say screechingly high-pitched, and Tess certainly would if asked.

"Hello, Evan. This is a…surprise."

Tess heard the falter and grinned. Whitney had just taken in Evan's new appearance.

"When you couldn't find room in your schedule, I decided to make room."

Oh, good. He was being strong and forceful.

"Why don't we plan to get together next week for a nice, long visit?"

Shouldn't there be some kissing going on? These two. Tess rolled her eyes. With the way Evan looked, Tess expected Whitney to buzz one of the secretaries and tell her to hold all her calls. Tess would have.

"Now works for me."

Good man, Tess thought.

"I see." Whitney huffed. "If you can wait until I drop these off with Miranda, I can give you a few minutes."

Well, that was big of her. The door pushed all the way open and a petite, suit-clad woman with white-blond hair in a flippy cut walked out.

So that was Whitney. Why did all the tall men go for short women?

Whitney went into another cubicle office and returned moments later. As she walked back, Tess got a good look at her face. Tiny was her immediate impression. Tiny nose. Tiny mouth. All to go with her tiny voice. Tess supposed some men might find that attractive, but Evan?

Whitney didn't spare Tess a glance as she entered her office. "All right. Here I am. Now what's this all about? Your parents are well?"

His parents? She hadn't seen Evan for weeks and she wanted to talk about his parents?

"They're fine. Currently on a cruise. I wanted to talk about us."

"Evan." Big sigh. "I do not want to have this discussion now."

What was there to discuss? After the reception Whitney gave him, she was surprised Evan was still there.

"You might not, but I do."

Go, Evan.

"It is not appropriate for me to conduct personal business at the office."

Clearly, the woman was no longer interested in

him as a romantic partner. Why didn't she just cut him loose?

"You can manage this once—there were enough times when you conducted business during our personal times," Evan said.

Tess heard a sigh.

"Evan, what has happened to you? You look…"

"Like eye candy?" he supplied.

Tess clapped her hand over her mouth.

"I was going to say scruffy."

There was a silence and Tess winced.

"And you like it." Evan's voice was low and throaty.

"No. I don't like it at all."

They'd veered off topic and Tess figured Evan was having second thoughts about his appearance.

"Why not?" he asked.

"Really, Evan."

"You're right. It doesn't matter."

"Of course it matters! People see you and connect you with me."

So hurry up and disconnect, already.

"I can see you won't bring up the subject, so I will. Where do we stand, Whitney?"

"I really don't have any more time right now." Her voice sounded like one of those yippy little dogs. Yip, yip, yip.

"Then give me the short version."

"This is about sex, isn't it?" she asked.

A beat passed. "Not with you."

Whitney might have gasped but it was drowned out by Tess's own gasp. What was he doing?

"Oh, Evan. I think I understand." Her voice was full of high-pitched sympathy. "Flashing your arm muscles, the tan, the tight jeans…you…you're coming out, aren't you?"

Omigosh. Tess held her breath and waited for the explosion.

"*Tess!*" Evan roared.

Tess scrambled up from the chair and dashed into Whitney's office. "Okay, this is not going very well. Time out." She actually made the T sign with her hands. "Whitney, we need to establish a few things. Number one, you and Evan are kaput. The relationship is over. You are no longer boyfriend and girlfriend. You aren't going steady, you're no longer dating, but you can still be friends."

"Who *are* you?" Whitney asked.

Evan did the honors, biting out the words, "Whitney, Tess. Tess, Whitney."

"And?" Whitney stared at him.

"And what?"

"Who is she? What is she doing here?"

"She's…" He looked at Tess.

"An interested party," Tess supplied.

Whitney's eyes narrowed. "I'll just bet you are. Are you responsible for that?" She wiggled her finger up and down at Evan.

"Yeah." Tess sauntered over to Evan and wound her arms around his. "And he's *so* not gay."

"What was I supposed to think? He looks like one of the Village People."

Evan pulled his arm from Tess's. "I told you," he grumbled.

"You do not look like a Village Person, you look hot," Tess reassured him.

"The Village People looked hot," Whitney said.

"Moving *on*," Tess said. "The point here is that Evan stood by you while you suffered from the world's longest case of jet lag, and now it's time to resolve things between you."

"Where did you find her?" Whitney asked Evan.

"In a bar," he answered, which let Tess know he was still mad about the Village People crack.

Fine. If he wanted to go down that path, then they'd go down that path. "Yeah, he picked me up a couple of days ago," Tess said. "I was his waitress." She gave him a gooey smile. "Look, honey, it's almost time for our forty-eight hour anniversary."

"You are not helping," Evan murmured.

"Sure I am," she chirped. "We've established that you two are no longer an item and all that's left is to say goodbye."

Only nobody said goodbye. What on earth were they waiting for? Tess glanced up at Evan and saw that his gaze was fixed over her shoulder. She turned around and saw Whitney gazing soulfully at Evan.

"Evan?" she whispered.

And then Tess saw that she had greatly underestimated Whitney. The woman could cry on command. Her eyes—blue, but squinty—filled with tears.

Oh, it was an excellent performance.

"Whitney, I'm sorry."

"Evan!" Tess snapped her fingers in front of his face. "Out."

He took a step and it wasn't toward the door. Tess pulled on his arm. "I want to speak to Whitney in private. Girl talk." She pushed and tugged.

"Tess—"

"Evan." She gave him a meaningful look.

"Tess?"

"The sooner you go outside, the sooner we can get your computer," she reminded him.

"Oh, Evan!" Whitney added a sniff.

"Whitney…"

"Evan, tell her it's been great and you'll remember her fondly and get the hell out of this office!"

Evan gave a decisive nod. "Goodbye, Whitney."

Tess closed the door behind him. Whitney was dabbing at the corner of her eyes. "You are good," Tess told her.

"So are you."

"Thanks. I can understand how you kept him dangling for two years, but I don't understand why."

"Convenience. And no matter what you think, I do like him."

"You know, I actually understand," Tess told her. "Right man, wrong time."

"I think so." Whitney leaned against her desk and glanced off to the right. On the wall was a calendar featuring scenes of London. June was Big Ben. In fact, the picture was taken from the same angle as the

Big Ben in the framed photo on the shelves next to it. Whitney was in that one, wrapped in the arms of a man. A man who was not Evan.

"Okay, well now it's time to throw Evan back into the pond. You don't want him and keeping one of the few genuinely nice, decent guys out of circulation when you really didn't want him is a crime against the sisterhood."

"What sisterhood?"

"The sisterhood of single women, of which you and I are members."

Whitney shrugged and returned to her desk chair. "You're not his type."

"No, I'm not." Tess grinned. "But it'll take him at least a week to figure that out."

Whitney's phone rang, so Tess held up a hand and left the office.

Evan was not happy. He slouched against the hallway leading to Baby Lawyer Land and scowled. In other words, looking exactly the way Tess had wanted him to look.

She smothered a smile. "Ignore Whitney. You look great. Every woman in this place checked you out."

He straightened. "And apparently some of the men, too."

Tess laughed, but Evan didn't crack a smile.

"Okay, where's your office?" she asked when they were back on the street.

"First, clothes for you." And the look on his face said that it was time for revenge.

"Oh, puhleeze. I'll just pretend I'm there for an interview or selling something or from the plant maintenance company—you've got one of those, right?"

"I think everyone waters his own plant," Evan said.

In the end, Tess relented, which was why she currently wore a navy blue suit. Oh, yes. Knee-length, straight skirt and prim white blouse and all. Tess hadn't planned to wear a blouse because the jacket collar was high enough, but Evan had been adamant.

Tess was horribly overdressed, not to mention far away from fashion's cutting edge, but there was no way she could convince Evan. And wool in June in Texas? Forget it.

Even worse, while she was trying on suits, he bought a new golf shirt and threw away the black T-shirt.

At least he kept the jeans.

They'd parked in an underground parking garage near the store. Tess looked exactly right exiting from the staid car. Evan looked as if he'd borrowed his parents' car.

"Hey, while I'm buying a new car, let's get one for you, too," she said.

He beeped the door shut. "Why?"

"This does not fit your image."

"It doesn't fit *your* image."

"Duh."

"Besides, the limo picks me up, anyway. How's that for image?"

"Good point. I forgot about the limo."

"Yeah, the driver picks up the management team and a few others, and we have a morning meeting in the car. The neat thing is that the driver, usually a trainee or a Bartholomew kid, gets to hear how the management of the company works. I absorbed a lot when it was my turn as driver, which is what Henry wants."

Not bad. Not bad at all, Tess thought. The company sounded like an interesting one to work for. It was the first positive thought she'd had about the corporate culture in over ten years. "Everybody is on vacation, so what's Quatro doing with himself?"

"Employees who win sales prizes get the use of the limo for a night on the town while Henry is on vacation."

"What fun. I like that idea."

They were nearly to the employee entrance of the store. "The offices are overhead," Evan told her. "Let's go over your story again—you're from Global Independent Marketing and you are here to pick up this week's marketing stats."

"Why wouldn't you just e-mail them to me?"

"I can't e-mail. I'm locked out."

"I meant…where are the stats?"

"There are no stats." Evan looked very irritated. It was probably the new shirt. The old one had been a lot softer.

"That's just your excuse. But it's unlikely you'll be challenged."

"Even when I walk out with a laptop?"

"Tess! That's what the briefcase is for." He handed the big black, unfeminine case to her. "You put the laptop in that. Now pay attention."

She hefted it. "And nobody is going to search my briefcase?"

"No!"

"Your place is an industrial spy's paradise."

"Just go in, look like you know what you're doing and get my laptop."

"Roger that." Tess gave him a snappy salute and pushed open the doors to Bartholomew's Best corporate headquarters.

7

THE PANIC HIT HER with a suddenness that took her breath away. The sounds, the smells, the beige-and-gray machines, the tweedy industrial carpet. Chairs on rollers, putty-colored cubicles...the glass walls of the fortunate few with offices. The muted tapping of computer keyboards. It all came back to her so unexpectedly, Tess had to consciously command her lungs to breathe.

Nothing like this had happened when they'd gone to visit Whitney so she hadn't expected her reaction now. But then, she'd been with Evan, who hadn't looked the slightest bit officey, and she'd worn her Tess, woman-of-the-alternative-world clothes, and the carpet had been plush and sound-absorbing.

The law offices had looked more like a hotel than the average office. Than this office. Maybe that was it, or a combination of the two.

Whatever, the closed-in feeling was back in full force. Tess's heart raced. Her lungs wouldn't fill completely. The panic took up too much room, and she couldn't get enough air. Pressure built in the center of her chest, right between her breasts.

Doom. She was doomed.

You are having a panic attack. Stop it. But knowing what was happening—that she wasn't going to have a real heart attack—didn't stop the symptoms or the queasy feeling that too much adrenaline brought. It never had.

But she wasn't going to leave this time. Tess exited the elevator, the office key Evan had given her biting into her palm. She gave a vacant smile to a young woman coming out of the copy room, and, following the directions Evan had drilled into her, strode purposefully down the hall in the direction of his office.

Striding felt good and used some of the excess adrenaline, but the feeling of doom persisted. She could never go back to this life. Never. In fact, it was all she could do to make herself stay here now.

Bartholomew's Best had the same gray-blue and oatmeal color scheme that her father's office had. The way half of modern offices did. Blue was supposed to be soothing or something.

Tess was not soothed, but she was determined to see this through. She forced herself to breathe and to concentrate on getting Evan's computer.

Afterward, they were going back to his house where Tess would sit on the sofa with a wet washcloth over her eyes and sip a glass of wine as she directed Evan in how to cook their dinner.

Yes. He would cook. He owed her. She would hold to that thought.

Her hand trembled with emotion and excess energy as she tried to fit the key into the door. She prob-

ably should have checked to see whether it was unlocked first.

"May I help you?"

Tess dropped the key.

The copy room woman had followed her. Younger
than Tess first thought, maybe intern age, she wore
a close-fitting wrap top and geometric-printed flared
skirt. That was *silk* skirt and top, not navy blue wool.

"Thanks, no." Tess picked up the key. At least
Evan had let her keep her own stylish shoes. "I'm
from Global Marketing and I need some stats that are
in Evan's office. He's on vacation, but I'm not."

"Yeah," the woman said.

If she stood there and watched, then Tess wouldn't
be able to get the laptop. "He works so hard, I can see
why his uncle had to force him to take the time off."

"Oh, I know," the young woman said. "The tim-
ing is lousy, though."

"Tell me about it. I have to turn in my report by
the end of the month and I can't wait until he gets
back. Bartholomew's isn't our only client." It was
amazing how easily Tess could speak the language
after all this time. Even though she was making it all
up, it sounded good.

"Yeah, well, I wish Evan *were* here. Everybody is
just freaking out about the rumor."

Tess looked at her. "What rumor?"

"The Alliance rumor—that Alliance Department
Stores is buying Bartholomew's Best."

"I hadn't heard that one." Her heart still pounded,
but it had slowed.

"Two Alliance guys were looking around in here yesterday. Cute."

"Really." Tess unlocked the door. Was this old news, or something Evan should know?

"Oh, yeah. They had that shaggy hair and nice bods." She clutched her copies to her chest. "Great smiles, too."

Tess tried for a casual tone, difficult with the adrenaline still zinging around her system. "You think they'll be back?"

"I dunno. It's kinda weird since Mr. Bartholomew and the others aren't here. I can't believe he'd sell the store and not be here."

"It's probably just a rumor." *Don't get involved. Don't attract attention. Just get out of here so you can breathe normally again.*

"Except there's a guy downstairs taking inventory with Mr. Shutz. And of course, there's the meeting."

"You'll probably find out everything then." Tess didn't ask about the meeting because she didn't think the character she was playing would and this young woman was talking *way* too much. Tess didn't want to get her into trouble, but she was going to have to tell Evan about the rumor.

"Maybe that's when they'll offer to buy our stock," the young woman confided unwisely. "I've only got ten shares, 'cause that's what we get when we start here, and I just started, but wouldn't that be cool?"

"Unexpected money is always cool." Tess still had all her unexpected money. She'd refused to spend any of Henry's money on the retro eighties' power suit, and had made Evan pay for it. He could have it when she finished here. She didn't want it.

"Hey—where did you get the key?" the woman asked after Tess opened the door.

Talk about a belated sense of security. "From Evan, and I had to beg. Nobody here will take his calls, so that's why I had to come by." Damn. The woman followed her into the office.

"Oh, wow." Papers were spread everywhere. Piles of papers. Hadn't he heard of electronic data? And what was with the mess? Tess wouldn't have expected it of Mr. Prissy Closet. "He acted like the information was on his desk," Tess said. "Wanna help me look for it?"

"What are we looking for?"

"Copies of the actual field data—the surveys from our field personnel. I prefer to analyze from the source rather than rely on the statistics he e-mails me."

Was that not great? Her response had covered both e-mail and hard copy. Evan had better have picked out some good wine.

"But aren't you the one who gives *him* the data?" the woman asked.

Didn't she have a job to do? "And I do, but we compare raw marketing data from other sources, especially if it differs by more than four percentage points."

Tess's mind buzzed. She just opened her mouth and all this stuff came out. She sure hoped her brain didn't short-circuit until after she had Evan's laptop.

They'd been gingerly lifting layers of the papers

when Tess had a brainstorm. Unfortunately, she didn't have a cell phone. "Hey—would you call him and ask him where *exactly* on his desk the files are, or if he's scanned them into his laptop? If he has, maybe I should just bring the whole thing to him. I don't have his number with me."

"Sure."

Tess caught the expression of relief on her face at the thought of letting Evan know someone was in his office. *You are so good.* The woman in the cute outfit looked up Evan's number somewhere and came back to dial from his office.

While she was out, Tess stuffed a few papers into her briefcase so it wouldn't look totally empty.

"Yeah, she's here. Okay." The woman held out the phone to Tess.

"Hi, Evan."

"Did you get caught?"

"Yeah, I'm here in your office and I don't want to disturb anything. Do you remember exactly where you left the info?"

"She's there with you, right?"

"Yes."

"Is my laptop there?"

"Yeah, it's right on your desk. So you did scan the hard copy?"

"Uh, yes?"

"Okay, that would probably be easier. Thanks." She hung up the phone. "He says just to bring the laptop. He can print a copy for me. And that'll hold me for now."

"Oh, good," the woman said.

As she spoke, Tess casually plopped her briefcase on top of the stacks of paper and slipped the slim little notebook computer inside. Smiling determinedly, she closed the briefcase. "Thanks." Tess waited for the woman to exit, and relocked Evan's office.

Then she fixed an image of a scowling, unshaven, ripped T-shirt clad Evan in her mind and escaped.

"TELL ME EXACTLY what she said again." Evan was in the kitchen doing things he thought he'd never to do a naked chicken while Tess lounged on the sofa with a glass of wine in one hand and holding a wet washcloth across her eyes with the other.

She told him again and she was very patient about it. Of course that was her second—or was it third?—glass of wine.

"And there were papers all over the floor of my office? The *floor*?"

"Stacks. Your desk, too."

Evan had been in the middle of something when Henry's order to leave had come through, but he wouldn't call his office an unreasonable mess. And stacks, plural, on the floor? Someone else had been in his office.

He stepped to the door of the kitchen to ask Tess if she'd noticed what kind of papers were out, but at the sight of her pale face and clenched lips, he chose not to.

Something had spooked her in the office, and he didn't think it was sales rumors.

And he couldn't find out about those because Tess had stuffed his laptop under the sofa pillows and wouldn't give it to him until he'd finished with this stupid chicken.

He could hardly stand it. E-mail was so close at hand. And this line of garbage Donna, the new hire, had fed Tess... Not good.

And another thing—as though he needed another thing—while he was glad Tess had retrieved his computer, he was concerned about how easy it had been for her. Once she'd got past the guard at the bottom of the elevator bank, which hadn't been difficult at all, then she'd been home free. But security issues were for another time and another battle, Evan feared. Henry was entirely too trusting and had way too much faith in his fellow man—and woman.

So. Back to the chicken. He'd now cleaned it and thrown out disgusting body parts.

"Put the giblets in a saucepan and boil them for stock," she said from the sofa.

Giblets, he assumed were the disgusting body parts he'd just ground up in the disposal. Saucepan? A pan was a pan in his book. Stock? Who needed stock? He'd lived this long without stock, he'd survive.

"Too late," he called back.

"Did you season the cavity?"

"Yes."

"Pat the outside dry?"

"I rubbed it dry." This wasn't a chicken spa, or anything.

"Rub some olive oil over the skin."

Good grief. "Do we have olive oil?"

"Yes."

At least Tess was sounding more relaxed. She'd been white when she'd emerged from the building and had been very quiet on the way back here.

"Okay. Should I put on a CD with sounds of rippling water or ocean waves so the chicken can relax while it cooks?"

"Ha. Don't forget that you're turning the oven back to three hundred and fifty degrees after ten minutes. Set the timer."

He wasn't sure how the timer worked. He'd just have to remember.

This was not the way he'd visualized the evening unfolding. He'd planned to unfold into Tess.

He was a free man. Whitney was out of his life without so much as a twinge on his part, or her part, either.

Okay, to be honest, the whole "coming out" misunderstanding bothered him. He'd thought he was being a gentleman by not pressuring her. And work had suppressed his less-than-gentlemanly urges anyway, so it had been a while since they'd been, well, urged. Which brought him back to tonight, in which he'd envisioned a teasing ride home and some clothes-tearing as soon as he and Tess made it inside the door.

That had not happened. There was no atmosphere of sexual desperation. There wasn't a sexual anything going on and, whether he wanted to be or not, he *was* a gentleman and was not going to pounce on a woman who was having issues with something that required her to numb herself with alcohol and wet linens.

"See the rice mix?" she called in a languid voice.

He looked around for the box. "Uh-huh."

"Follow the directions."

He flipped the box over and found more of the simple directions like those on the brownie box, and the brownies had turned out good. Well, hey. Cooking wasn't so hard. Why did women make such a big deal of it? After the rice, there was going to be some vegetable from a bag—he voted for the green beans—and all he had to do was microwave that.

"How's it going?" It sounded like *howzhit goin'*.

"Great." Evan dumped the rice in a pan with water, turned the heat to High, and snagged some cheese and crackers. Tess needed something in her stomach.

He headed for the sofa. "Tess." Evan swept aside the *TV Guide*, the paper, a couple of remotes and a stack of marble coasters that nobody ever used, and sat directly on the coffee table by Tess's head.

"Wha'?"

He took the tilting wineglass out of her limp grasp. "Want to tell me what's up?"

"No."

He sliced a square of cheese off the end of the yellow chunk, stuck it on a cracker and waved it under her nose.

Eyes still closed, she opened her mouth and he set it on her tongue.

"Tell me what's up."

She crunched and swallowed. Her chest rose as she took a long, slow breath and let it out in a whoosh. "Panic attack."

Evan had heard about those, though he wasn't personally familiar with them. He took her hand and held it loosely. "You okay?"

"I will be."

"I mean without the wine."

"Eh." She waved her other hand from side to side and then removed the washcloth. "Being in the office triggered it. Whitney's place didn't bother me, but the Bartholomew's Best office had a similar color scheme to my dad's and it just hit me. All at once."

Evan struggled to understand. This was Tess. He *had* to understand. "Being in an office environment triggers a panic attack?"

She regarded him with heavy-lidded eyes, and this time they weren't filled with lustful thoughts. "Yeah. I thought I'd gotten over it."

He rubbed his thumb over her knuckles, wishing he knew what more he could do. "If you'd told me, I would have never asked you to—"

"Shh. I know. It's a been years since I had one."

"Did they start when your father died?"

She kept looking at him with her eyes half-closed, and her soft, sensual mouth, a mouth he wanted to kiss more and more with each passing moment, pursed. "You're a nice guy, Evan."

He reminded himself that she was *not* looking at him with lust. "That's me, your all-around nice guy."

"I meant it in a good way. Your family is good people. You're also hot."

"Hey." He gave her hand a little squeeze. "You don't have to say it if you don't want to, and you don't have to pretend to feel something now that you don't. I'm not going anywhere."

"I know. You're still hot, even in that preppy shirt."

"Shall I rip its sleeves off?"

"Uh, no." She tugged gently on the hand he held, drawing him to her.

He tilted forward, understanding that she wanted him to kiss her.

And he wanted to kiss her, a lot, actually, but not when she was like this. "I can wait," he whispered.

"But maybe I can't," she whispered back.

She looked very convincing, and he so wanted to be convinced, but the rice chose that moment to boil over, rattling the pot lid and hissing as the water hit the hot element. Evan took off for the kitchen and turned off the burner.

The interruption was for the best, though maybe not the best for the rice. He stared at the pan, with the white goo running down the sides, shrugged and put it back on the burner.

Oh, yeah. He was supposed to turn down the oven and he'd nearly forgotten. That was close. Evan adjusted the temperature and when he walked back into the den, Tess had put the washcloth back on her eyes.

Evan returned to his spot on the coffee table and took her hand again. He sat there, content to hold her hand and wondered why he was content to just hold her hand.

Evan sat there and watched Tess and considered his life up to this point. Then he considered what his life would be after this point, specifically after the week or so Tess said she would stay. There would be more time off and then he'd go back to work.

Could he go back to work as though he'd never known her? Did he want to?

Before he could decide on the answer, Tess abruptly started talking. He thought she might have fallen asleep.

"Right after my dad died, I quit school to keep my job with his company. I was really good and worked a bunch of crazy hours because it was like if I succeeded, then I'd make him proud and people wouldn't forget him and I put all kinds of pressure on myself and one day," she gulped a breath, "I had a panic attack and thought I was having a heart attack, just like he did."

She spoke so quickly that her words were echoes by the time Evan absorbed their meaning.

"The next day, it happened again. And the day after that. Antianxiety medicine worked for a while, but I guess my body got used to it or something because the attacks returned. And then they happened when I got out of my car in the parking lot. And then, in the morning before I left for work. So I took more medicine, until it happened again. But the medicine wasn't effective anymore and I couldn't make myself get dressed to go into the office. My mom didn't understand. After Dad's death, she'd soldiered on—even started her own interior design business—why couldn't I?"

Evan didn't think she expected an answer, but he tried anyway. "Have you thought that it's because you're the one who found your father? Maybe these attacks are a form of shock and grief."

"Oh, absolutely. But, here again, knowing what it is doesn't lessen the feelings." Tess pulled her hand away and sat up, catching the washcloth as it fell. "After a while, the thought of any job or making any decision triggered the panic. So I told myself I didn't have to do anything and I just packed some stuff and got in my car and started driving. When I ran out of money, I'd get jobs. For a while, I'd get sales jobs in a mall, but after one retail Christmas season—no way. Too much pressure. So, I started waitressing. If I had trouble finding a job, I'd run up a tab I couldn't pay and offer to work it off. That's how I landed at Temptation in Kendall. And that's the longest I've been anywhere." She was silent.

"Tess—"

She interrupted him with a shake of her head. "I wanted you to know, okay? And maybe some of this is because the bar is closing. I felt comfortable there. I should give Cat a call and let her know where I am. I want to go back before the place is torn down."

SHE'D NEVER TOLD another human being all that—not even the therapist.

"Aw, Tess," Evan said and her heart blipped.

She stared at him. Yes. There it was. Definite blipping.

This was very inconvenient. Her heart hadn't blipped since she'd been a college freshman. But that blip had turned into a bloop and she never thought to blip again.

This was probably just leftover adrenaline from her panic attack.

She and Evan spent a long time just looking at each other. He'd laced his fingers through hers and was just *there*.

She'd freaked out and he'd taken it all in stride. Yeah, he'd made a few clueless guy moves—well, only one, when he'd shown *way* too much interest in his laptop when Tess was just trying to breathe—but, to be honest, once he'd realized she was in true distress, he'd been...incredible, now that she thought about it.

Tess hadn't leaned on many people in her life. Something clicked and she saw a part of her childhood in a new light. She'd *never* leaned on anybody. She was an only child. Her parents weren't the coddling types and she'd been encouraged to be independent. Good grief—did she even know *how* to lean on somebody?

There was Evan, right in front of her, looking very leanable, even in the stodgy green golf shirt. Discounting the beard, from the waist up, he looked like he was about to tee off. But from the waist down, whoa mama. She grinned.

He smiled back. Yes, the beard was coming along nicely. "What?"

"You. Your outfit. It's you. The mix—the responsible man and the off-duty bad boy. I like it. Not at the same time, though."

He cleared his throat. "I haven't had an opportunity to demonstrate my bad-boy qualities."

"Oh, sugar, I walked down the hall behind you at Whitney's. That was pure-grade, natural-bad-boy walking."

He looked pleased, though she could tell he was trying not to. "The boots changed the way I walk."

"You should wear them all the time. Even when you wear those suits."

"Maybe I will." His eyes scanned her face.

Tess figured she was looking better. She felt better.

She owed him. Her teasing had held an implicit promise of fun and games, and she'd intended to honor the promise.

He'd been very good about waiting, but then he'd waited for Whitney, the yippy-dog woman.

The man must be desperate, and yet he held her hand and waited.

Blip, blip, blip.

Tess unlaced their fingers and slid down the sofa until they were knee to knee. "You're too good to be true."

His eyes darkened. "Not good. I'm having very not-good thoughts."

Tess put a hand on either side of his face, running her thumbs across his rough jawline. Then she drew him to her and gently kissed him.

She tasted chocolate—he'd been sneaking brownies. The thought made her smile as she broke the kiss.

"Nice," he murmured, his eyes still closed.

The kiss had gone over so well, she kissed him again, liking the feel of his mouth and the cautious restraint he demonstrated. Oh, yes, she felt the frustrated little quiver in his jaw and the way he adjusted the pressure of his lips and their movement to match hers.

She felt a vibration and knew he'd suppressed a moan.

Or…or was that her moan? If it wasn't then, it would be soon.

What had been intended to be a sweet, you're-a-great-guy-and-you-are-going-to-be-oh-so-happy-later kind of kiss had changed into a happiness-now kind of kiss.

Actually, it changed when tongues had become involved. When had that happened?

Who cared? Not Tess, not when Evan shuddered and slid his hands around her waist.

This knee-to-knee position was awkward and didn't provide nearly enough body contact.

Evan clearly had the same thought because just as Tess scooted across the gap, he cupped her bottom and she landed on his lap, where she wasted no time in fitting herself close to him.

"Tess." He exhaled her name with his eyes closed. "This is—"

"—really great," she finished for him. "But I can make it better." Tess began undoing the buttons of the hated white blouse she wore.

Evan stared, his chest rising and falling, as her fingers moved from one button to the next until she slipped the thing off her shoulders and tossed it to the side. She'd kind of expected him to help, but maybe he was more visual than tactile.

She was reaching for the clasp on her bra when the grimace on Evan's face stopped her.

"S-slow down."

She could do slow. Since she'd been wearing a tank top when they'd started out this morning, this wasn't one of her lacy hoochie-mama bras, but she'd make do with what she had.

Holding his attention, she caressed her collarbone and drew her fingers across the modest dip of cleavage, blazing a trail for, say, his tongue.

Evan swallowed. "You probably shouldn't do that." He spoke through gritted teeth and his hands were clenched into fists.

She was witnessing a terrible internal struggle. "You don't sound too sure."

"Give me a minute."

"Okay." She tugged his shirt out of the waistband of his jeans. "In the meantime…"

He took her hands in his. "Tess…"

"Oh. Oh, right. The medical preliminaries. I forgot. Look, I talk a good game, but I'm extremely picky. Extremely. And I figured you, well, the Whitney thing…"

"You're right, but this is about you and the fact that you don't really want to be doing this and while I really, really, *really* want to be doing this, tonight is not the night. And as you pointed out, it has been a really, really, *really* long time for me, so I've reached my limit here." He smiled crookedly at her.

Tess gazed at him for a long moment as a strange warmth spread through her. "So, you're saying that if, for instance, I asked if we could just cuddle, you would?"

"I've been wanting to cuddle you ever since you walked out of the Bartholomew's Best building." He drew his arms around her and nudged her to rest her cheek on his shoulder. "Everything is going to be okay," he whispered and just held her.

The warmth flooded her, relaxing her muscles until she melted against him. A lump formed in her throat and Tess did something she hadn't been able to do even once after that terrible day eleven years ago, or in all the days since—she cried. She cried for the father she'd lost and her failure to achieve a success he would have admired. She cried for the type of mother she'd wanted, but never had. And then she cried because Evan held her in a way no one ever had.

8

SHE'D BOO-HOOED all over Evan for hours. How sexy was that? Probably sexier than the swollen eyes and blotchy face she had this morning.

Tess awoke on the sofa, wrapped in an afghan that screamed gift from a grandmother. It was white with poinsettias on it.

Evan was nowhere around, but Tess could still feel his arms around her. He had stamina, she'd give him that.

Forcing open her eyes, she saw the box of tissues on the coffee table. Next to them was a bottle of aspirin. What a guy.

Tess grabbed the bottle and headed into the kitchen for some water. The kitchen was pristine, reminding her that midway through her rendition of Niagara Falls, Evan had insisted that she eat. They'd had scorched rice and dried-out chicken, and it was the best meal she'd ever eaten.

Tess swallowed the aspirin and started a pot of coffee. After that, she looked in the freezer for ice and settled for a bag of frozen green beans, which she put over her eyes when she got back to the sofa.

It didn't take a therapist to know that the release had been building for a long time, and Tess sincerely hoped all her issues had been resolved.

She so owed Evan. He deserved a medal, or at least the best sex of his life.

And she was going to see that he got it.

EVAN HAD SPENT the night in Tess's room, but without Tess. And honestly, even Tess, hot as she was, would have trouble overcoming the pink-and-white girlie decor of his cousin Jos's former bedroom.

But Jos's room had a desk and an Internet connection and Evan didn't want to disturb Tess once she'd finally fallen asleep.

He'd been profoundly moved by the depth of her grief and honored that she'd opened up for him. He didn't want her feeling embarrassed and backing away from their emotional connection, either.

The thing was, he thought he was falling in love with Tess Applegate. She'd fit into his life as neatly as a missing puzzle piece. Now he had to convince her that he'd fit into her life. That would take some doing, since Tess kind of made up her life as she went along.

Restless, Evan had taken his laptop upstairs last night to check e-mail and see what he could find out about those rumors Tess mentioned.

He hadn't planned to stay up all night, but that's what he'd done. And the more he dug, the more he found. He contacted seven people before one— Donna, the intern—would give him a workable password. And she had the lowest security clearance—and he used the term *security* loosely.

Something was going on and he wasn't sure what. This morning, a whole bunch of folks were going to find e-mails from him—with Donna's name listed as the sender—in their in-boxes. He hoped at least one would read what he had to say and get back with him.

Evan smelled coffee. Tess must be awake. He ran his hand through his hair and over his jaw.

The beard bothered him. Of course, if it turned on Tess, he'd keep it and gladly.

She was still on the sofa when he went downstairs.

"Hey. I smelled coffee. Can I steal some?"

"Go for it," she said from beneath a bag of green beans.

Right. He'd forgotten about the green beans last night. He'd also forgotten about the chicken and the rice, but they'd already been cooking.

He grabbed a mug of coffee and sat on the table, just as he had last night. "How are you feeling this morning?"

"Embarrassed and tired, but the storm has passed."

"Good."

"And you are one lucky man."

"How's that?"

"I am very grateful and I plan to demonstrate my gratitude in many creative and numerous ways."

Evan tried hard to force polite words of denial out of his mouth, but, well, she should be grateful. She'd scared him, damn it. And even with her face covered by green beans, he felt a powerful tug of attraction.

"Hmm. You missed your cue to say something encouragingly sexy. It's the green beans, isn't it?"

Evan laughed.

"I look awful," Tess told him. "I saw my reflection in the microwave. It's best if you don't have this image of me in your brain."

The way she looked now couldn't be worse than she'd looked with her face contorted by grief and all the other junk that had come spilling out of her.

Tess needed loving, pure and simple, and Evan was more than willing to provide the loving.

But after a nap.

"Evan?"

He sipped his coffee. "Hmm."

"Not awake yet?"

"Uh…"

She slipped the bag from her face. Her eyelids were swollen and her face was red from the cold.

"Well, hey, you've looked better," he said.

"Heaven forbid you should be one of those guys who tries to flatter his way into my pants." She studied him. "Those circles are back under your eyes. You've been up all night."

He nodded and drank more coffee. Though he hoped she wouldn't for a few hours, in case she wanted to express her gratitude right now, he wanted to be ready to accept it.

"Did I keep you—?" she began uncertainly.

"No. I was on the computer."

"Working?"

"Just chasing down that sales rumor you heard."

"And?"

"There are things that don't add up. I have some calls out."

As if to prove his words, the phone rang.

"You're supposed to be on vacation," she warned as he went to answer the phone.

Evan listened, then brought it to her. "Quatro? Something about car shopping?"

"Right." She winced. "I thought we could all go help me find a new car today and then have lunch at Jos's restaurant. She's back on the day schedule."

He wanted to, he really did, but he didn't want to miss any phone calls. It was hard enough to find someone to go against Uncle Henry's strict "hands off Evan" policy. But Tess, with her puffy eyes and vulnerable expression, wouldn't take that well as an excuse.

"I can tell you're tired," she said. "And I want you good and rested, so I'll go out with Quatro and you take a long, restorative nap."

She spoke to Quatro and handed him the phone when she was finished. "About tonight…"

"Yes?"

She smiled and he thought about canceling some of those e-mails. "I'll take care of everything, and I mean *everything*."

Blood pounded through his tired brain. "What exactly do you mean by *everything*?"

She licked her lips and he stared at her mouth, watching it form the words, "Anything you want."

They stared at each other and Evan was thinking

that they shouldn't wait for tonight when the phone in his hand rang. He checked caller ID and exhaled. "Marcus is calling me. Finally." He answered the phone as Tess slipped away.

This was great. He'd get the rumor situation straight and then he'd sleep and take vitamins and shower and figure out whether he was supposed to shave and then maybe he'd take more vitamins. And then...

And then he tuned in to what Marcus was saying.

TESS HAD A GREAT DAY and looked forward to a greater night. She didn't buy a car—couldn't decide if she wanted a convertible, cute as it was, or not. Leather in the hot Texas summer sun was nothing to fool around with. Quatro didn't think it would be that bad, but he wasn't wearing shorts or a skirt. So he suggested she rent one for a week to see how she liked it.

It was a clever idea and she told him so. At that point, he looked at her in a way that told her he was getting a crush on her, which she was going to have to, well, crush.

His mom joined them for lunch and then Tess went shopping in her bright red, two-seater convertible.

Frankly, it had been more fun in the limo with Quatro.

Her first stop was the lingerie department of an upscale department store. Not Bartholomew's Best. They didn't carry lingerie, and Tess wouldn't have shopped there anyway, even though she was spending Henry's money.

She bought the wicked and wickedly expensive designer stuff she'd seen in magazines. The kind with price tags that made her wonder if the women were insane to pay that much.

No. They were not insane. The finest silk and lace cupped her breasts and whispered over her hips. Just wearing it made her feel...aware. So she wore a set out of the store as she spent the rest of the afternoon shopping for Evan.

He was in for every man's fantasy evening. Tess felt lighter, freer and happier than she had in a long time. Maybe ever, and she had Evan to thank for it.

Well, maybe Henry, too, she thought as she paid for a new set of eight-hundred-thread-count sheets for Evan's bed. While she was shopping, she picked up a bottle of the cognac that Henry liked so she could give it to him with the CD Quatro had made of her mangling a few songs.

She bought gourmet food for light, but sustaining snacks, candles, and massage oil.

By four o'clock, *she* was ready for a nap.

Tess found her way back to Evan's house and parked in the driveway. Her little two-seater was packed with stuff, including a couple of plants because she'd decided Evan needed more plants, more living things in his house. And maybe a pillow or two. She hoped he didn't mind, not that he'd notice anything she didn't want him to notice once she took control of the evening.

Tess made four trips from her car to the kitchen door. She made enough noise that Evan had to know she was back, unless he was still sleeping.

She grinned. Time to wake him up.

Tiptoeing into his room, she saw the empty bed. He must be upstairs.

Tess headed upstairs and found Evan staring at the computer monitor and typing furiously. Papers surrounded him and his hair stuck up at odd angles. The bed she'd slept in that first night was undisturbed. Oh, he might have made it, but what guy would have taken the time to arrange the pillows and stuffed animals in exactly the same way she had?

"Evan."

He jumped. "Tess!" He closed his eyes and his shoulders sagged. "You startled me. Hang on." He typed some more. "I'm IMing some people."

"You're talking to them on the computer?"

He glanced up. "Yeah."

In that instant, she saw the focused gaze, the dark circles and felt the nervous energy. She also saw the four empty cans of Coke.

"You haven't had that nap yet, have you?"

Without taking his gaze from the computer, he shook his head. "I'm just about to."

"It's after four-thirty."

At that he stopped typing and blinked at her owlishly. "Oh, man." He scratched his jaw. "This thing is driving me nuts."

The beard didn't look as attractive to Tess as it

had yesterday. Even with the spray tan, the beard didn't go with dark circles under his eyes and the air of exhaustion.

"Why don't you go take a shower and shave it off? You'll feel better."

"Yeah."

"And you can have a short nap while I make a few preparations."

"Sounds good." He gave her a quick, impersonal smile as he stood.

He wouldn't smile that way if he could see her underwear. Tess considered showing him, but elected to follow him down the stairs. Later.

While Evan was in the shower, Tess restrained herself from joining him—not that he'd asked her—and changed the sheets on his bed. The rich coffee color contrasted nicely with the beigy neutrals in the room. She draped the silk lounging pants she'd bought across the chair and a spa-type terry cloth robe across the foot of his bed. Beside the bed, she placed the rolled-up terry massage mat she'd bought. Couldn't have any oils messing up the new sheets.

On the nightstand, she put a black bowl that would hold heated stones. That didn't leave much room for candles, but she managed to squeeze two musk-scented pillars on the edge. On the other side of the bed, she left a sack of props she'd bought. She didn't know Evan's style, but that was part of the fun to look forward to.

She proceeded to put pillows around and add candles to the living room. Lots of candles. More candles than she'd ever had going at one time in her life. It always looked so good in the movies. It wasn't nearly dark yet, so Tess closed the blinds and headed for the kitchen.

She was moving fast, but everything was taking longer than she'd anticipated. Seduction was exhausting. She wanted to get ready herself.

"I wasn't sure what to wear." Evan stood in the doorway of the kitchen. He'd opted for the lounge pants and bare chest.

"Good choice." As she stared at him, Tess was hit with a barrage of feelings, of which desire was only one.

He'd shaved and the circles under his eyes were back, but the fake tan made him look better than he probably felt.

That and leaving off his shirt.

Tess was revising the evening's timetable when Evan padded across the kitchen tile and casually captured her mouth in a kiss.

Captured was the word. Pressed up against his bare chest, his hands warm against her back and his mouth open against hers, Tess had no doubt who was in charge of this kiss. She might be running the evening, but he was all man. All impatient man.

He broke the kiss, pressed his lips to her forehead and rubbed her shoulders as he looked at the grocery sacks on the counter. "What's going on here?"

I'm having a mini-meltdown, that's what's going on.

She loved, loved, *loved* kisses like that. Casually

carnal and possessive, as though he had the right, which he did. Very self-assured manly kisses, the kind that came from very self-assured and manly men.

Okay, she'd admit it. Evan was more man than she'd thought. Sure surprised her. She blinked as he walked over to the counter, the lounge pants riding low on his hips.

"Can I help?" he asked.

Oh, yes, oh, yes. "You can find some CDs and put them on. I'll get some things going in here and shower and change."

"I can give you a hand in here. Are there boxes with directions? I do a mean box with directions."

She laughed. "Yes. On the counter, but tonight I was going to do everything for you."

He gave her a lazy smile. "I'm sure you'll make it up to me."

Oh, she was *so* going to make it up to him.

KISSING TESS had revived him, but it didn't know how long the surge of energy would last. Stupid. Stupid. Stupid not to sleep.

Evan opened a box of frozen bacon-wrapped jumbo scallops and read the directions. Broil in pan. His kind of directions.

He poked around in the other sacks and found caviar, which he'd always thought was overrated, but then again, Whitney had told him that the really good stuff was like tasting heaven. Hmm. Didn't want to be thinking about Whitney, and he had his own idea of what heaven tasted like, so he put the jar of caviar in the pantry. It looked lonely there with nothing but some cans of soup, pickles, crackers and sodas to keep it company.

Smoked oysters. He could take or leave oysters. He opened the square tin and picked them out of the oil. Tess must be into seafood.

There were some frozen empanadas, but they were supposed to be baked, so they'd have to wait until the scallops were done.

He found strawberries and chocolate dipping sauce that could be warmed in the microwave. That sounded good.

According to the directions, he had to wash and dry the strawberries before dipping.

Okay, fine. It kept him occupied and awake and not obsessing over Tess and what she was doing, which was showering. Showering meant she was naked. Right now. And wet. Right now.

He stifled a yawn. This was not good. Thinking about Tess should not prompt a yawn.

He shook his head, dropped to the floor for a set of push-ups, ate a couple of oysters and hoped for the best.

She'd bought champagne, but he was thinking that alcohol wasn't such a good idea tonight. He wanted to be alert, he wanted to remember and savor every minute of Tess.

In the living room, he tuned the radio to a soft rock station and lit the candles she'd placed around.

"It looks nice," she said from behind him.

"You're the one..." he trailed off as she came into view.

Her hair hung softly to her shoulders. Her make-up was muted and her outfit was...was... "Wow." He swallowed. She had layers of see-through stuff on in a dark blue that reminded him of the navy blue suit he'd made her wear. He saw strings, as if she were a living package of sorts, and a garter belt and stockings. He knew what a garter belt was, but had never seen one in person before.

"I didn't know if you were into women's lingerie," she said.

"You mean wearing it?" His voice was an octave higher than normal.

She laughed, a rippling musical sound that was surprising since she couldn't sing. "No. Me wearing it."

"I thought I was a skin man, but I could get into fancy underwear."

She walked toward him. "You're allowed to touch, you know."

Touch Tess. "I'll explode if I do."

"Oh, well, too bad. It's not nearly time for explosions." She flashed him a triumphant smile and walked away, trailing some exotic scent after her.

He watched her and zeroed in on the fact that she was wearing a thong beneath the garter belt. Her tush was nearly naked. And what a tush it was, too.

He watched her walk on feathered high-heeled shoes, watched the muscles in her legs and hips move and felt all nonessential thought processes close down. Much more of this and it would be man-woman-mate-now.

He was going to sit on the sofa and calm down before he embarrassed himself.

She returned moments later with the food tray he'd started and two filled champagne flutes. Yeah. He changed his mind. Champagne would calm him down.

"The scallops are nearly done. I turned them over. Do you like seafood?"

"Yes." He didn't know. He didn't care. He just didn't want her to stop moving or go away.

She bent over and set the tray on the coffee table and noticed him staring at her breasts. It was hard not to. They were…there. In front of him. Eye level.

She put an oyster on a cracker and fed it to him. "You like?"

"Uh-huh." He tasted nothing.

"I'm talking about this." She gestured to herself.

"Uh-huh."

Tess handed him the champagne flute that he drained without tasting.

She sat next to him, drawing up her legs. "You see this little string here?" Her fingers fluttered near her throat.

"Uh-huh."

"If you pull it, the robe will open." She smiled.

He pulled.

She inhaled.

He stared. The fabric veil fell away from her skin

and he had a clear view of what had been underneath. It was as though she was wearing a lace tray that served her breasts.

"Today, I learned that expensive lingerie is worth every penny."

"Uh-huh."

"For instance," she continued, scooting closer to him. "Take lace."

Who cared about lace?

"I always thought lace was scratchy. I never wanted it next to my skin."

Evan's gaze drifted to her skin. It looked very soft. Scratching it would be very bad. He was glad he'd shaved.

"But this lace is so soft. As though I'm wearing nothing. Nothing at all."

Maybe to her.

Her voice dropped to a purr. "Don't you want to touch it and feel how soft the lace is?"

"Uh-huh." But he couldn't make his hands move. After days of restraining himself, something had short-circuited in his brain. Could sexual frustration cause strokes?

When he didn't move, Tess reached for his hand, kissed the tips of his fingers and drew them across the lacy edge of her bra. "Doesn't that feel good?"

"Uh-huh."

She gently withdrew her hand, leaving his fingers. Evan traced the rippled edges, barely registering the line where lace ended and skin began.

Tess inhaled, causing his fingers to dip lower.

In a far corner of his dimly functioning brain, he was aware that while she'd said she'd do everything, he was pretty sure that acting as though he'd been struck dumb was not earning him any points.

But he was struck dumb because right behind the scrap of lace and satiny material was Tess—and not very far behind, either.

He gently drew his index finger over the upper curve of one breast, dipped into the cleft between them and traveled across the other side.

She bit her bottom lip. "Soft, isn't it?"

"Uh-huh."

She drew a deeper breath and the lace shifted just a few millimeters, but enough to reveal a darkening curve.

Evan swallowed as a freight train roared through his head. His hand trembled with the force of his emotions, which wasn't cool at the moment. Plenty of tremble time later.

He withdrew his hand. Tess blinked and released her lip, the beginning of uncertainty causing a crease between her eyebrows.

Evan wanted to reassure her, to tell her that he just wanted her so damn much he was afraid of succumbing to certain animalistic behaviors that involved ripping, tearing and plunging.

Instead, drawing once more on his self-control, he leaned forward, caught the scalloped lace edging in his teeth and folded it down, pressing it into place with his tongue.

Tess moaned and shifted on the sofa.

Evan curled his fingers into fists as he felt the darkened skin pucker beneath his tongue. He delved deeper beneath the edge until he found the hardened tip and lifted it out with his tongue.

Tess gave a shuddering gasp, but when he closed his lips over her and grazed her with his teeth, she just plain gasped. And when he created a gentle suction, she exhaled a moan.

"O-okay." Hands on his shoulders, she pushed slightly. "I'll admit I was a little concerned there for a moment, but not so much now."

Evan stared at her and tried to form coherent, noncavemanesque thoughts.

"I had other things planned—" her voice was strained "—but let's go to the bedroom now."

"Uh-huh."

Taking his hand, she drew him to his darkened bedroom.

He couldn't wait. "Tess."

"Wait."

No.

She bent down and retrieved something which she unwrapped and spread on his bed. "I'm going to give you a nice, relaxing massage."

He didn't want a nice massage and it wasn't going to be relaxing because he sure didn't see how she expected him to lie on his stomach.

"Let me take off those uncomfortable pants so you can lie down."

He quirked an eyebrow upward. "That won't help."

She stopped, her hands on the drawstring waist.

"Well. I see. Try sitting on the edge of the bed with your back to me."

That wasn't going to help, either, but he sat.

"Great back, but your muscles look tense."

Duh.

He heard her opening something.

"I've got some oil here, so my hands will be smooth and slip easily over your skin."

She rubbed her hands together and he smelled some dark, faintly smoky scent. Though he wasn't a smoker, it make him think of cigarettes and sex.

Behind him, Tess moved closer and placed her hands on his shoulders.

His muscles tensed involuntarily, and desire coiled low and tight in his belly.

"Relax," she whispered.

Right.

But she persisted, rubbing and kneading his shoulders and the corded muscles at the side of his neck. A groan escaped. "That's good." He indicated his right shoulder. "It's sore from using the computer mouse."

"You are supposed to be on vacation."

"I know."

"Close your eyes and relax, dammit."

Smiling, Evan closed his eyes and tried to relax. Tess worked his shoulder with both hands and, though he would never have believed it, the tensed muscles began to soften.

He tilted his head back and Tess worked the area beneath his ears. "You've got great hands," he breathed.

"Can you lie down now?"

"Oh, yeah." Eyes still closed, he stretched out on his stomach.

Tess moved her hands in long strokes on either side of his spine. Heaven.

He was barely aware of her straddling him and how a few moments ago he would have been unbearably excited by that. Now, now everything was moving in slow, comfortable motion.

He inhaled and let the problems with the store and rumors and being really good for Tess just escape with his breath.

Tess found places in his back—little pockets of resistance he didn't know were there—and massaged all the tension out of them. He was loose. He was relaxed. He didn't have to move. He didn't want to move. He might never move again.

And for the rest of the night, he didn't.

9

EVAN ASLEEP. Tess couldn't believe it. Here she was, in mid-seduction, and the seductee was on the verge of snoring. Not attractive.

She stared at his lovely back, oiled skin gleaming in the candlelight, and contemplated waking him up, or at least taking off his pants. He'd be *soooo* much more comfortable. Slipping her hand beneath him, she sought out the drawstring on the silk lounge pants. *Note to self: elastic.*

She found the string and pulled.

Nothing. Well, the pants loosened, but there was not one little, tiny flinch from Evan. Tess drew her fingernails slowly over the skin of his belly. Either he was not ticklish in the slightest, or he had sunk to the deepest stage of sleep.

It might have given another girl a complex, and Tess would admit to being miffed. She understood that he was tired, but had he taken a nap to overcome his tiredness? No. Had he had the opportunity for a nap? Yes. And what had he chosen to do to prepare himself for their night of sensual delight? A night with *her*?

Work.

Tess did not think she was overreacting here. She might not be Miss Universe, but she knew chemistry when she encountered it and they had enough chemistry to bottle and sell in Bartholomew's Best. And it had all been silently acknowledged and delayed and had been simmering to an explosive boil.

Tess poked Evan. Nothing. Desire had left the building.

Tess leaned down until her lips were next to his sleeping ear and crooned, "Evan, if you don't wake up, I'm going to sing to you all night."

A sound that wasn't quite a snore was his response. Oh, okay, it was a baby snore. Kinda cute, actually. But no. Cute wasn't the order of the night, here, and neither was snoring.

Tess could have joined him on the new sheets on his bed and taken a little nap herself. But for one thing, she couldn't sleep, and for another, she was mad.

She told herself it was her own fault for insisting on giving him a massage when things had been going oh-so-swimmingly in the living room, but she'd already skipped a few steps—one of which had been removing the scallops from the oven.

Few things smelled worse than burned seafood.

So, between venting the smoke and opening windows and doors to air out the place, no, she wasn't sleepy.

She put away the rest of the groceries, blew out the candles and watched some television, but in the end, she opted for the room upstairs instead of joining Evan in hopes of some midnight delight.

Once in the girlish bed in the room lit by the computer monitor's glow—until she turned it off—Tess thought about what had happened.

This was a replay of her childhood—her father putting work ahead of everything else, her mother working because her father was working and Tess being left to raise herself. Oh, yeah, poor her. She'd dealt with it, but that didn't mean she wanted to recreate it.

Evan was supposed to be on vacation. True, there was the whole rumor thing and, to be fair, Tess was the one who'd told him about it. But he should have taken a nap! Right now, he could be having mind-blowing sex with her and he was oblivious to the world.

All that wasted potential made her crazy. It was a bad idea to stay here in his house. Tess wasn't quite ready to leave Austin yet—it was a cool town and she might even stay here a while, but she wasn't going to be staying at Evan's place any longer.

She couldn't stand it.

EVAN SLOWLY CAME TO, disoriented because it felt as if he was lying on a towel. He blinked at the dark sheets, and realized he was on the massage mat on his bed and that Tess must have changed the sheets. He hadn't noticed the night before. Evan reached out and fingered the material. Oh, man. The stuff felt like silk. Knowing Tess, it might even *be* silk.

He turned his head, hoping to find her there and was disappointed, but not surprised, when he didn't.

Briefly, he reviewed the events of the previous night even as he registered an odd odor. The massage oil and something else. Something unpleasant. Something burnt.

He winced as he remembered the scallops. Smiled as he remembered the massage that was the cause of the burned scallops. And...groaned when he couldn't remember anything after the massage because there *hadn't* been anything after the massage except him falling asleep. Tess had not slept with him in any sense.

This was not good. Evan pushed himself off the terry cloth and saw that his chest and one arm had tiny pinpoint-sized dimples all over. Not attractive.

He stretched, realizing that he felt better than he had in ages. There's irony for you.

He had to find Tess, but not looking like this. And he was going to have to woo Tess. It wasn't going to be easy. Evan figured he'd start with coffee—she really liked her coffee. And maybe a shower in hopes that the moisture would even out his skin.

There was no sign of Tess in the living room, so she'd clearly spent the night upstairs. His computer was also upstairs and he couldn't very well go in there and check his e-mail when Tess was sleeping. That would not go over at all.

At this point, he shouldn't even be *thinking* e-mail.

He started the coffee and took a shower, noting that he felt ready-to-take-on-the-world better. If only he'd felt this way last night when he should have been taking on Tess.

He headed toward the kitchen, intending to take a cup of coffee up to her, when he tripped over the first inkling that Tess wasn't going to be as understanding as he'd hoped.

A familiar blue duffel was at the foot of the stairs. Next to it was a garbage bag that also looked familiar. But then again, a garbage bag was a garbage bag.

Evan looked inside and yes, those were Tess's clothes. Damn.

He started to call her name, but first got a mug of coffee with sugar as a peace offering.

"Tess?" he called when he was once again at the bottom of the stairs.

Tess, dressed in shorts, a tank and flip-flops, appeared at the top railing. "Oh, good. You're awake."

Just the way she said it told Evan he had his work cut out for him. Ignoring the duffel and the garbage bag—and the suitcase she was bumping down the stairs—he held out the mug of coffee. "I was bringing you some coffee."

She continued down the stairs.

"With sugar, the way you like." He smiled hopefully.

Tess snagged the mug on her way past him. "Thanks." After propping the suitcase next to the pile, she sipped at the coffee.

Her tank top was navy blue and he wondered if she'd chosen it to deliberately remind him of what she'd been wearing when they'd last been together.

He took a step toward her. At the movement, she glanced up, freezing him in place.

Nope. Not on purpose. This was going to require

serious groveling. "That was some massage last night. You're quite talented. I relaxed so completely, I fell asleep." He grinned. Again, hopefully.

He grinned alone.

"You should have woken me," he continued.

"I tried."

"Maybe you should have tried harder."

"I did. You passed out from exhaustion."

"I wouldn't say I was exhausted."

"I would. The first thing I thought about you that day in Temptation was here's a guy working himself into the ground. After you had a couple of nights' sleep, you were looking pretty good, but then you worked yourself silly and didn't have the reserves to bounce back."

"I feel bounced back now. And I know it was the massage." And the sleep, but that was a sore subject.

"Great. Glad I could help."

He took a step toward her. "Tess, I'm—"

"Ready now? Sure you don't want to check your e-mail first?"

"I'm sorry." He figured it was the first of many repetitions.

She set the coffee mug on the finishing curve of the bannister. "So am I. We would have been great together."

She headed for his bedroom and hope surged, as well as other parts of his anatomy. "I left some of my things in here."

How long was she going to act like this? Irritation flared briefly, and or maybe it was frustration. She was looking great this morning. No sleep wrinkles marred her skin and because of the short shorts and scooped neck and bare arms, he could see a lot of skin. Not the most interesting parts, which he had not seen last night, either.

"Tess, I didn't commit some horrible crime, I just fell asleep while you were giving me a massage. You should be flattered." As groveling went, not so good.

"Do not make this my fault!" She marched around the bed. "I made it my fault when I was growing up."

"What are you talking about?"

"My parents. It's a classic situation kids get into— I thought if I were perfect, they'd pay attention to me and give me their approval. But I wasn't perfect and my dad's job was more important than I was." She reached for a sack by his bed. "My mother...I guess I can understand why she buried herself in work. But I am not going to compete with a man's job ever again."

"Tess, you aren't competing."

"You're right. Too bad for you. You should see the tricks I had in my bag." Lips tight, she reached into the sack and pulled out what looked like a miniature feather duster. He could take or leave feathers.

"Yes, I know. Cliché city. I do have all the standards in here. But they could have been fun." She up-ended the sack. "Chocolate body paint, honey dust, lotion that warms the skin, scarves, handcuffs, flavored condoms, ribbed condoms, tickler condoms, knobbed condoms, glow-in-the-dark condoms, and the jelly fun pack." She picked it up and looked at the purple, green, yellow, red, pink and blue objects encased in a bubble pack. "I don't know what some of this stuff is."

His blood had begun pounding. Energetic, rejuvenated blood. "I do."

"Well." She raised an eyebrow. "Still waters and all that." She shrugged. "Too bad." Gathering up all the toys, she said, "I'll just be all ready for someone else."

Evan didn't know if it was her words or the offhand tone that inflamed him more. Or maybe it was the jelly fun pack.

"No. I want a second chance. And if you like second chances, I can guarantee a third and a fourth chance."

"Evan..." She exhaled and began rolling up the massage mat. "You're a nice guy. But it's not happening. You'll get over me."

Evans did not feel like a nice guy. When she started to leave, he grabbed her arm. "Aren't you going to give me something to get over?"

She looked startled.

"Oh, yeah." He took the mat out of her limp grasp. "Did you really think you could spend days winding me up and I would let you just walk out?"

"I—"

"Sure you did." He grabbed her other wrist. "Because that's what a nice guy would do." He pulled her to him. "But that's not what *this* nice guy is going to do."

And he kissed her.

SHE WAS ON FIRE for him. Instantly. Regrettably. And surprisingly. She usually didn't respond to caveman tactics, but she was responding now.

This behavior was not to be encouraged. She should let him know that she didn't appreciate being manhandled and she would, just as soon as he took his tongue out of her mouth.

In the meantime, as long as it was there...

Really, she didn't even have to kiss him back because he was kissing hard enough for both of them. Surprisingly enjoyable.

Then he wrenched his mouth from hers before she was ready. Here was her chance to tell him just what she thought of him, except that she...forgot.

So when he growled—yes, growled—a demand that she kiss him, she, well, did.

She couldn't have him thinking she didn't know how, could she? And it was best to leave with him wanting more, wasn't it? So she'd just demonstrate what he'd be missing after she walked out. It had to be a memorable kiss so he'd suffer and memorable kisses weren't quick, so giving him a really good memory was going to take some doing, er, kissing.

Tess stood on tiptoe and wrapped her arms around his neck and made sure her clad-in-expensive-silk breasts were pressed against his clad-in-stupid-golf-shirt chest.

She'd show him, yeah she would. She'd kiss him silly and when he was weak with desire, she'd break the kiss, casually tell him to, uh, kiss off, and sashay out the door with her extra-tip walk.

Tess knew how to make an exit. Her extra-tip walk would be his last image of her. Forever burned in his retinas and all that. And she would put this brilliant plan in play as soon as she was sure of the weak-with-desire part.

On *his* part.

Because, he'd now come on board this kiss and Tess was afraid that sashaying didn't work very well on wobbly knees.

She'd have to be strong and take control. Think analytically and plan her moves to achieve the maximum effect. On Evan.

He cupped the back of her head and tilted slightly, changing their alignment from pretty darn good to damn near perfect.

His tongue stroked hers and it felt so...wait a minute. Her tongue should be stroking *his.* She was the one in charge here. She was the one who was going to leave him gasping.

She pulled his tongue deeper into her mouth, sucking gently. And when he tried to withdraw, not so gently. And rhythmically. Ha. That'd teach him.

Evan planted both hands on her Southern cheeks and pulled her toward him, fitting her pelvis between his thighs. It was a pretty darn good fit there, too.

Okay, so the arena had broadened. Tess was still on her tiptoes, so she lowered her heels and slid slowly down his body. He gasped because it felt so good. Or, she assumed the rubbing felt good to him because it sure did to her. So good, she did it again and again. And, okay, so maybe he wasn't the only one gasping.

Maybe she didn't care.

Evan stepped forward. She stepped forward, too, but not far enough to catch her balance and fell backward onto the bed.

Evan followed, capturing her hands and holding them above her head, his hard male body pressing her into the expensive cocoa-colored sheets.

Breathing heavily, he grinned down at her, just out of kissing reach.

Okay. Okay, she could still be in charge. She'd just flip him over, straddle him, kiss the daylights out of him, and then escape while he was still recovering. That's what she'd do.

Tess tried scooting her leg out from beneath Evan, but all she accomplished was to have him settle between her thighs.

Leverage. She needed leverage.

Evan dropped his head and softly kissed the side of her neck, nibbling his way along her collarbone, his tongue flicking out and dipping into her cleavage beneath the scoop neck of her tank.

Her arms went boneless. So much for leverage.

This time, when he raised his head, his look had turned predatory.

Good. She had him right where she wanted him.

"I'm sorry I fell asleep." His voice was raspy and she could barely make out the words. "Last night, if you'd jumped my bones the instant you got in the door, I guarantee you would have been happy."

"Aren't you assuming a lot here?"

"I assumed nothing. You've been asking for it for days."

Tess hated it when a man got sexually smug, unless he was entitled and Evan, in spite of his current position, wasn't yet entitled.

"I have not been asking for it! I've been telling you *you* were going to get it!"

"And yet..." He shifted her wrists to one hand.

Oh, right, like one of his hands could hold both hers. She jerked her arm, surprised when nothing happened. She pulled again, harder. And still her wrists remained above her head.

Oh. Oh, drat it all, she *liked* it. And he knew it, too.

He grinned and skimmed his free hand under the hem of her top, playing with the skin above the hip-hugging waistband of her khaki shorts.

His touch wasn't light enough to tickle, just enough to sensitize.

And distract. He was distracting her from her goal, which was...was something.

His fingers ventured higher. Okay, she'd remember her goal in a little bit.

"I worked all night because I believe something is going on at Bartholomew's Best and I need to find out what."

"I can't believe you're talking about *work* at a time like *this!*"

He just smiled and let his fingers wander higher to tease the lower edge of her new bra. "Patience, Tess. I need to explain a few things."

Did he think she was *eager* or something? "I'm a very patient person. I am patience personified."

"Really." He slipped a finger beneath the edge of her bra and caressed the underside of her breast.

She wiggled beneath him. "Hurry up and explain whatever you need to explain and then... then..."

"And then?"

"Just hurry."

His fingers stilled, which wasn't exactly what she had in mind.

"I got the blue duffel, too."

Tess stopped squirming and blinked. "Too?"

"Yes. When I was off making my dot-com fortune, I also lost my dot-com fortune. The company sank so fast it hit bottom and kept going. Henry bailed me out. No questions. No lectures. He said, 'I give these to people who have dreams. Sorry I was late.' It was a second chance for me. I paid off my debts and when I came back to the company, it was because I wanted to. So, Tess, I feel protective of Henry and the family business. I've expected something like a takeover attempt because we're vulnerable." He kissed her forehead. "And though I didn't expect you, I'm vulnerable there, too."

"Odd, since I'm the one pinned down." Her heart was blipping and she didn't want it to. She didn't want to be vulnerable, either. Tess imagined her heart being tough, like leather. That way, it didn't hurt when it got kicked around.

"I wanted you to listen."

"I listened."

"I want you to understand."

"No," she said softly. "You want permission to put work first. And I will never give it."

"And I will never ask it." At which point, he kissed her. Hard.

Which was totally not fair because Tess had been considering what he'd said and, on the surface, it appeared he was reassuring her. But when taken another way, it sounded ominous, which was probably why Evan kissed her—to keep her from thinking.

It worked.

"You're trying to distract me." Her voice was a little too breathy to pull off the commanding tone she was after.

"Not at all. If I were trying to distract you, I'd do something like this." Evan barely moved his fingers and flicked open the clasp on her bra.

"It took me longer than that to get it fastened!"

"I'm motivated."

Tess jerked her arms, more for form's sake than because she really wanted to free them.

Evan surveyed her, then tugged at the hem of her top, pulling it up. She expected him to bunch the fabric around her neck. But Evan neatly snagged her shoulder straps, stretched the whole thing over her head without touching her face and then kissed her as he replaced the hand holding her wrists and managed to remove the tank all at the same time. An exquisitely efficient move.

And just like that, Tess was half-naked in Evan's bed.

He probably hadn't even noticed her hot pink bra.

"I knew you'd be beautiful," he murmured and took the tip of her breast in his mouth.

Okay, so she'd show him the underwear later. Before she sashayed out, she'd toss it over her shoulder. Yeah. It would make a great visual... "Ah!" A shudder ran through her. "You...you..."

"That was a little love nip to see if you were paying attention."

Tess's mouth dropped open.

Evan stared down at her, his eyes dark with intent.

It occurred to Tess that, perhaps at this *précise* moment, arms pinned, body pressed, and half-naked as she was, that she might not actually be the one in charge.

As they stared at each other, Evan began idly flicking her other breast with his fingers.

Tess wanted to buck her hips. She wanted to draw his mouth to hers—or somewhere—but if he thought she'd go nuts with him just casually watching and apparently not involved *at all*, well, no. She simply wouldn't respond. She wouldn't. He was supposed to be weak with desire. That was the goal, she remembered now, though it was a miracle she did.

They continued to stare at each other and he continued to caress her. Tess gritted her teeth with the ef-

fort not to move. Her breath came in tiny shuddering puffs, so she tried not breathing.

She wanted to move. She was desperate to move.
She was…she was weak with desire, dammit!

Sweat beaded in her hairline and she had to breathe.
Too bad it sounded like a gasp, because that would just
feed his male ego and she couldn't have that.

When, exactly, this had become a force of wills
and why, she didn't remember. Still holding her gaze
with his, he lowered his head, stuck out his tongue
and licked her.

She groaned, a long aching sound. That was it.
That was just it.

"Evan McKenna, you will get your clothes off
right now, reach your hand into that sack and grab a
condom of any color shape or flavor and get inside
me within the next ten seconds, or I will spend the
rest of my life making you regret it."

He ripped off his shirt. "All you had to do was ask."

"After that crack, you'd better be the best I've
ever had."

He ripped off his jeans. "I will be."

He was so outrageously self-confident that Tess
was intrigued, in spite of herself. "Well," she eyed
him as she shimmied out of her shorts. Okay. Okay,
this, well, this was going to be good. "You've certainly got the potential, but what makes you so
sure?"

He rolled on a condom. Not colored, for the record. "Because you love me."

Tess's mouth worked, but nothing came out. He

thought—the man was absurd. "You…you think I love you."

"Oh, yeah." Evan laid her back on the pillows and positioned himself between her unresisting thighs. "Which works out really well, because God knows I love you." And he slid home. "Sweet," he breathed into the side of her neck.

"You—you just told me…"

He raised himself on arms that shook and met her eyes. "That I love you, yes."

"And…" She swallowed and licked her lips, forcing herself back to the conversation and not to think about how wonderfully he filled her. "Could you just move a little bit, just to, ah…"

Her head fell back and she bit her bottom lip as Evan slowly withdrew and pushed in again.

She whimpered and didn't care. "This love thing," she gasped. "You said that I…that I—"

"Love me, too."

Love? How dare he presume…

Evan gave her the sweetest smile. An understanding, patient smile—though it didn't stop him from rocking into her a couple of times—a smile that waited for her to catch up.

Love? Love. *Love.* "Omigosh, you're right!"

With that, he picked up the pace. "I'm glad we finally came to an agreement. Let's come to another one."

Tess used her newly freed arms to hold him close and proceeded to have the best sex of her life, just as he'd promised.

10

LATER—ACTUALLY, MUCH LATER—and after enough best-sex-of-her-life repeats so Tess knew it wasn't a fluke, she asked Evan, "How did you know I loved you? I didn't know I loved you."

"Yes, you did. You just didn't want to admit it."

She'd give him a pass on the smug smile. "And you knew this how?"

"You were so angry, for one thing, and so ready to run away, I knew you were scared. You weren't scared of me, so I knew you were scared of your feelings."

"That makes me sound really wimpy."

"No. Love is a huge responsibility and you don't want responsibility. You aren't afraid of love, you're afraid of the expectations that go with it."

"Not all of them." Tess dabbed at a smear of left-over body paint on his abdomen. "For instance, I expect you to do that thing you do with your tongue a lot. I'm sure not afraid of that."

He dipped his head to her belly button. "This?" He vibrated the point of his tongue against her skin. "Or this?" He headed lower and Tess quivered in anticipation.

Yeah, she loved him. So sue her.

"Well? I think I should perfect your favorite right now. Which is it going to be?" He grinned wickedly. "Only one…"

"Don't ask me to make decisions at a time like this!"

That would be the moment the phone rang.

They stilled.

Evan dropped a kiss on her knee and stood. "Don't, that's do not, repeat, *do not* turn this into a test. We've been in bed all day and it's nearly four-thirty. I should take this one since I let the machine catch the other two calls."

"What other two calls?"

"You didn't hear." He grinned. "You were busy. And you're noisy when you're busy."

She'd been busy a lot. When he left the room to answer the phone, she drew the sheet over her naked and sticky body. Maybe showering off the leftover body paint would be a good idea. In fact, Evan would join her once he told whoever was calling to get lost.

Tess stood in the shower and waited. Then she soaped herself. Evan could always soap her again.

And then she watched her fingers turn pruney and still Evan wasn't in the shower with her.

Finally, Tess dried off before she used up all the hot water and went to find Evan.

He wasn't in the living room. Apparently, he'd also answered the siren call of e-mail. That's where he was, at his computer.

Tess climbed the stairs to find him at the computer in Jos's room, just as she'd figured.

"Hey, babe." When she got within reach, he planted a kiss on her arm all without removing his gaze from the computer monitor.

"I waited for you in the shower."

"And I am sorry I missed that." He still hadn't made eye contact with her.

Mindful of his words, Tess tried not to let it bother her. "How about now? I think I missed a spot."

He didn't say anything.

"Right here." She took his hand and slipped it beneath her towel.

"Hmm," he said. He did manage to look away from the damn monitor long enough to send her a quick smile as he pulled his hand away.

Yes, *pulled his hand away from her naked flesh.* Still, she was going to be reasonable if it killed her. "Tell you what. I'll fix us something to eat while you finish up here."

"Thanks."

"This is not a test. This is not a test," she chanted as she went back downstairs. She pulled on her shorts and tank, leaving the hot pink underwear on the edge of the bed where Evan would see it. Now *that* was a test.

Smiling, she headed for the kitchen.

Half an hour later, Tess figured she was going to have to buy a computer so she could e-mail Evan herself. Instead, she fixed a plate of goodies and carried it up to him.

"Thanks," he said.

He was so polite. "Talk to me, Evan."

Shaking his head, he turned in the chair so his back was to the computer. "It's a hostile takeover. It's a damn hostile takeover. There's a shareholder meeting coming up in a few days. I'm still trying to catch up with all the family so they can vote against it, but because it's Bartholomew's policy to give stock to the employees, the family doesn't own majority." As he spoke, he wolfed down the food. She'd felt the same way because, other than the chocolate body paint, they hadn't taken time to eat today.

Okay, Tess, now this is a test. Her man needed her. Her man. She smiled, liking the sound of that. "How can I help?"

Evan put the plate on the floor and used both hands on either side of her face to draw her into a gentle kiss. "You're the best, Tess."

YOU'RE THE BEST, *this isn't a test.* She kept repeating the jingle as the hours slipped by. Tess's job was calling people and when the time got too late for calling, she studied employee stock holdings and pulled their phone numbers so she could begin calling again in the morning.

Throughout it all, she and Evan tried without luck to contact Henry or find someone who could. They were also hampered because Evan's relatives had scattered to the four corners of the earth for their vacations, a fact that Alliance Department Stores, the evil enemy, had known and was exploiting.

By midnight, she was ready to pack it in. "Come on and let's go to bed, Evan. To sleep."

"You go ahead. I'll be there in a little bit."

And how many times had she heard a variation of that? Did he have to use almost the exact words her parents had used? However, Tess was too tired to argue about it, so she headed for bed.

Sometime in the wee hours, Evan joined her. She roused enough to be aware that he'd spooned his body against her back and then went back to sleep.

THREE DAYS LATER, Evan's house was filled with more relatives than he'd seen at one time since Uncle Henry's sixty-fifth birthday.

Many were cranky since they'd been called away from their vacations. Honestly, these people were obsessed with their time off.

Tess had been great. Her voice had a new husky quality, roughened by repeatedly leaving messages on dozens of answering machines. They'd had zero luck with people returning their calls until Evan realized that his number was coming up on their caller IDs and Henry had asked people to refrain from talking to him.

Tess went out and bought a cell phone—something he couldn't believe she didn't already have—and once she used that phone, they had much better luck.

She'd been great. Fabulous. Understanding.

And mind-blowing in bed.

She was a little too quiet for him to have complete peace of mind, but she did spend an awful lot of time talking on the phone and, if he did say so himself, she was one satisfied woman.

The only tiny problem now was that Tess, after passing around plates of sandwiches and soft drinks to the crowd, had slipped away because she said it was a family meeting.

But he wanted her there. Someday, he wanted her to *be* his family. But he knew better than to pressure her.

Her look of shocked horror when he'd told her she loved him, and she realized he was right, was fresh in his mind. He'd have to go slow with Tess.

TESS SAT in the chair in Evan's bedroom and hugged her knees. She could hear everything that was going on in the next room. People—Bartholomew cousins, in-laws, second cousins, and virtually everyone except Evan's cruising parents and the upper management echelon—were there.

She listened as Evan explained what he'd learned and that Alliance was buying up little dribbles of employee stock here and there.

She listened to Evan's aunt and uncle argue with another relative about the legalities of a clause in the employment contract that would only allow stock to be sold back to the company. There wasn't one, so the argument was moot. But time-consuming. At this rate, she'd have to make another sandwich run.

The big sticking point was deciding their strategy for the meeting Alliance had called, conveniently during Henry's vacation.

This meeting was sounding more like squabbling. They needed an unrelated third party. They needed her, Tess decided with a sigh. How ironic that everything she'd learned in her old corporate life was going to come in handy now.

She took a deep breath, testing herself. So far, so good. No sign of panic. Must be the sex. There might not have been as much of it as there would have been if there hadn't been this crisis, but what the two of them had enjoyed had been choice.

She'd never had the emotional connection with another person before. Not even her parents, really. The amazing thing was that Evan sensed this and had been unbelievably understanding. Could she be any less understanding about what was going on outside the door?

C'mon, Tess. This is what being in a relationship is all about. She exhaled and stared at her knees. Good God Almighty, she loved that man. How had it happened?

Time to put up or shut up. Tess licked her lips and her first and second fingers and stepped into the room. And then she let loose with her bar whistle.

A startled silence greeted her. She may not be able to sing, but she could whistle. "I'm calling a ten-minute snack break. Everybody is to get up and walk around, get something to drink and have some cookies." Honestly, if they were going to act like a bunch of kindergartners, then she was going to treat them like a bunch of kindergartners.

The best part was that they did as she said without grumbling. Jos and Evan helped her in the kitchen. Well, Evan was mostly there to sneak a kiss.

"This is a mess," he murmured next to her ear. "And we're having generational issues. The board isn't here and the most senior people want to be in charge, even though they aren't the ones who are the most informed about this."

"I want to help." Tess handed him a cookie tray. "And not just by feeding hordes of your relatives."

He smiled and popped a cookie into his mouth.

"As you told them, your immediate problem is the employee meeting. If your relatives all turn up, Alliance will increase their stock purchase offer. And you could intimidate the employees. What you really want here is a postponement until Henry and your board returns."

"Exactly." Evan's aunt Linda reached across the open kitchen breakfast bar and took a cookie from a tray Jos was filling. "I knew you were smart. You'd have to be to work at Doyle and Taft."

"Doyle and Taft?" Quatro had followed his mother over. Now, he grabbed a handful of cookies. "Tess, you worked at Doyle and Taft?"

"Yes." She took a breath. It was a normal one and she smiled reassuringly at Evan, who was watching her closely.

"What's that?" Jos asked.

"*How* can you not know Doyle and Taft?" her brother asked her in disgust.

"It's a strategic planning and business management firm," Evan answered. "They analyze and advise on corporate policy, risk management, corporate structure and that sort of thing."

"They rule," Quatro said. "Literally. And they make a potful of money doing it. I can't believe you worked there."

Tess managed a smile. "Hey, Quatro, that'll teach you not to read page two of the reports."

"Didn't read page one," he mumbled.

"Did you?" she asked Evan. "Read page two of the report?"

"I may have skimmed it. What did you do for them?"

Tess was still breathing okay, so she answered him. "I gave presentations to potential clients. I was...really good at it until...until I left."

"Woo-hoo!" said Linda. "You're just what we need."

Evan broke in before Tess could speak. "We don't need to drag Tess into this."

"But she'd be perfect!"

Evan gave her another one of his heart-melting smiles—which usually got him some pretty great sex—and said, "She *is* perfect."

Tess sucked in a breath. "Perfection is a lot of responsibility."

"Perfectly stubborn sometimes," Evan amended.

Tess laughed. "Evan is protecting me because I...have issues."

"Oh, your dad. Right," Quatro said around a mouthful of cookie.

"It's okay, Evan," she assured him. "I want to do this. For me as much as for you, I think."

"You don't have to prove anything, Tess."

She scrunched up her face. "Yeah…I kinda do."

Evans's cell phone rang and he handed Tess back the cookie tray. She gave it to Jos, who took it out to the others, avoiding Quatro's reach as she did so.

"Hey, it's my parents." Evan stuck a finger in his ear and moved next to the refrigerator.

Linda touched Tess on the arm. "Don't feel you have to represent us at the meeting."

"Wow. And you don't even know about the panic attacks."

"So that's what happened." Linda made a sound of sympathy. "Okay, forget it. We'll find another strategy."

"I want to try," Tess said. "One of you can back me up and I'll leave if I have to. How's that?"

Linda smiled. "You really love him, don't you?"

"Can *everyone* tell?"

She nodded. "Pretty much."

"I couldn't tell."

"I know that, too!" Linda laughed. "This family sneaks up on you."

"Tess!" Evan stuck his phone next to her mouth. "Say hi to my parents."

His parents? Swallowing, she said, "Hi. Pleased to meet you."

There was a pause as the ship-to-shore communication kicked in. "Hi, Tess. Hello." They both spoke and she pictured them, cheeks pressed together sharing the phone. "We knew Henry picked a good one this time," Evan's mother continued.

"I can't sing," Tess felt compelled to tell these complete strangers who, just coincidentally, were Evan's parents. And by this time, she wasn't surprised that they knew about her.

"Does Evan mind?"

"Um, no."

"Then you shouldn't, either."

Practical bunch, these Bartholomews—or technically, these McKennas.

After saying goodbye, Tess handed Evan back the phone, completely won over by the fact that he had wanted his parents to talk to her.

Yeah. He was a keeper, all right.

TESS WALKED through the doors of Bartholomew's Best corporate headquarters and knew that Evan and his aunt Linda were right in the car with Quatro in case she needed them.

She had the backing of the entire Bartholomew clan. She was going to save their store. And she'd wanted to avoid responsibility.

She hadn't panicked yet, though. It was funny. Linda and Jos decided her panic was due in part to appearing in public in the hideous navy blue suit. They lent her a Pucci print shell to go beneath the suit in lieu of the white blouse and she was wearing Linda's lucky mating-lizards brooch. This was more like it.

Tess had prepared and practiced. She was ready.

It was perfectly natural for her heart to beat a little faster. Kept her on her game.

She slipped into the meeting room and marveled

at the gall of Alliance to hold a takeover meeting in the target's own offices.

The smarmy Alliance people ran the meeting and made their offer. A few employees asked questions about Bartholomew's Best's future and Tess listened to a bunch of garbage about changing with the times. Tess let them run on, gathering information and waiting for the most opportune time to speak.

She felt confident. She'd done this before and she'd been good. One of her specialities was analyzing people—honed, ironically, during her stint as a waitress.

When she judged the time was right—just before the vote to sell stock—she stood and was recognized. Very important point, that.

She took her time walking to the front of the room, turned and faced the gathering and asked, "And how does Henry Bartholomew feel about this?"

The room hushed and several people looked down guiltily.

"Henry Bartholomew—" began the Alliance rep.

"I have been duly recognized and have the floor," Tess interrupted him. "According to *Robert's Rules of Order*, I am allowed to speak. Since not adhering to *Robert's Rules* will nullify the proceedings, I know you'll hold your comments until I'm finished."

He nodded at her. Shaggy hair, or not, she didn't think he looked so cute.

"So, Henry Bartholomew doesn't know about this meeting, does he?" she continued. "And the board doesn't, either. By the way, does anyone know how to contact Henry?"

Tess studied the people who wouldn't meet her eyes. She scanned the shaking heads, ignored the murmurs and zeroed in on a man midway back who looked so miserably guilty, she almost stopped the meeting.

Tess had several possible ways she could take this, but the group seemed to respond to guilt the best. "You remember Henry Bartholomew, the man who signs your paychecks? Oh, and the man who gave you the stock you're so eager to sell. The man you're stabbing in the back."

Gasps. Excellent.

"We could use the money," somebody called out.

"Right," Tess said. "Most of you have your original ten shares of stock. Alliance is offering, what? Twelve-fifty? Maybe as high as fifteen dollars if you hold out past the first sell-off? So, we're talking a hundred and twenty-five dollars? A hundred and fifty?" She paused and made eye contact with as many as she could. "Integrity used to be worth more."

She thought she had them. "All I'm asking is that you take time to think. To wait. Table the offer and have another meeting with Henry and the board when they return from vacation. You owe them that."

People were nodding, except for the man she'd noted earlier. Tess took a deep cleansing breath. She could do this. Now for the call to action.

"Let's hear a motion to table the vote." Technically, she couldn't call for a motion, but she was hoping someone would speak up anyway.

Someone did. "Fine. We'll offer fifty a share," said the Alliance spokesman. "But it's a one-day offer. And the price starts dropping by the hour."

The room erupted. People pushed their way to the front.

The one thing Tess had been trying to avoid had just happened—Alliance had increased their purchase offer so much, people wouldn't wait. They wanted to sell now. They didn't want to give Henry a chance to talk them out of their easy money.

She'd failed. All she'd had to do was to get them to agree to wait to sell their stock until Henry got back and she'd failed. She drew a short breath. Spectacularly. Another breath. She'd let Evan and his whole family down.

Tess pressed her fingers to the growing tightness beneath her breast bone. It had been her responsibility to make this work. She swallowed. She'd let them down. They'd lose the store if enough people sold their stock to Alliance.

Evan would hate her. She'd lose Evan.

She couldn't breathe. She'd lose Evan.

Tess was in the middle of the mother of all panic attacks before she realized it. People were pressing against her and all around her in an effort to get to the front of the room and all she wanted to do was run. She had to get out of here, out of the building so she could breathe again.

Evan and Linda were a cell phone call away.

Evan. Tess couldn't even hear the crowd noise anymore. She had to do something to stop this mad rush of people. To make them stop selling their stock. To get them to listen to reason.

Fighting her feelings of impending doom, Tess stood on top of a chair and shouted, "Stop!" As if anyone was going to pay attention to her. "Listen to me!" Or listen.

She was going to faint and she had farther to fall now since she'd stood on the chair. It was like being on the little stage at Temptation the first time. She'd been nervous, but when she'd started to sing, she'd forgotten everything else but the power of the music moving through her. That power was what she needed now.

So Tess opened her mouth and began singing. She closed her eyes and sang to Evan. Their song. "IIIIIIIIEEEEEEEEIIIIIIIIIEEEEEIIIII…"

EVAN FIGURED it was bad if Tess was singing. He hadn't waited outside—did she really think he wasn't going to be right there for her? Besides, the security guard hadn't been there to stop him.

"YOOOOOOOUUUUUUU…"

The funny thing was, Tess had stopped the wild stampede to sell stock. When Evan slipped in the doorway, people were frozen in place, gazing at her with a kind of fascinated horror. And they didn't even have alcohol. A few left the room.

"EEEEEEIIIIIIUUUU…"

Evan made his way to the chair and laced his fingers through hers.

She continued singing. When she paused to take

a breath for the big finish, Evan said, "If somebody will move to adjourn, I'll make her stop. But as long as you're selling stock, she's singing."

"YOOOOOOOOOOOUUUUUUUUUUUUUU."

A motion to adjourn was shouted, seconded, there was a hasty vote ending the meeting, and the room emptied.

And Tess still sang. Evan was pretty sure the song was supposed to be over by now.

"Make her stop," the Alliance rep whimpered.

So Evan climbed onto the chair and kissed Tess into silence.

"YOU FOUND THE GUY in the meeting?" Tess and Evan were back at his house and she was wrapped in Evan's Christmas afghan on the sofa with a glass of herbal iced tea. "I *knew* he knew where Henry was."

"Yes, Tess," Evan said patiently.

She knew she kept asking the same questions, but she still felt rattled.

"And he said he'd contact Henry?"

"He said he'd contact the other ham radio operator on the fishing trip and ask him to give Henry the message."

"But you haven't heard anything yet."

"Because he might be out on the boat and not near his radio equipment."

Tess drew a deep breath. It was wonderful to fill her lungs again.

"But why are you worried? Tess. You did it."

She shook her head. "I *didn't* do it. They were endorsing those stock certificates as fast as they could."

"And you stopped it. The meeting was postponed until Henry gets back. He can handle things."

"I sang my way through a panic attack."

"Whatever works."

"Right." Tess was silent a moment. "But this isn't."

"What?"

"Working."

Evan regarded her for a moment, and then took the iced tea glass from her hand and set it on the coffee table. Then he unwrapped her from the afghan, took her hand and led her into his bedroom.

"You think sex solves everything, don't you?" she asked.

"No, but it's really far ahead of whatever's in second place." He sat her on the bed and removed her flip-flops.

"Evan, I can't do the corporate thing. I can't. Not anymore. I thought I could. And I was great as long as everything was going my way—"

"Lift your arms," he said.

Tess automatically lifted her arms. "But at the first sign of opposition, I lost it. But I know your family will expect me to go back to that life."

He pulled her T-shirt over her head. "Hey. Where's the fancy underwear?"

"I wasn't in a fancy underwear mood."

"I am. I'm totally into fancy underwear. That's hideous. Take it off."

"Evan…"

"I'll take it off."

Tess didn't resist. "Evan, have you been listening to me?"

"Yes. Corporate, no. Fancy underwear, yes."

"Your whole family is corporate."

"Lift your hips."

She shifted and he whipped off her shorts and underwear. "Evan, I can't stand by and watch you be all corporate and work yourself silly the way you've been, either. I *can't*. I won't."

"Can you watch me take off my clothes?"

"I'll force myself." She clearly wasn't going to convince him of anything right now.

He shucked his clothes in about two seconds and Tess decided they could continue the conversation later.

11

LATER TURNED INTO the next morning. And even though Evan had ignored the ringing telephone, Tess knew it was time for her to move on. Sure, the take-over attempt had been a special circumstance, but look at how quickly Evan had reverted to his workaholic self. It wasn't supposed to be a test, but it had been.

She began packing while Evan was in the shower.

"Tess!" Evan was dressed in shorts and, bless his heart, one of the T-shirts she'd bought him. His hair was still wet from the shower and he hadn't shaved yet. He looked really good, even though his tan had faded. "What are you doing? I thought we settled this."

"We had sex. We settled nothing."

The phone rang. Evan didn't even flinch. "We made love. There's a huge difference."

"I know. And...and it's because I love you that I'm moving on. I can't fit into your life here."

"So we'll make a new life."

"Bartholomew's Best is your life."

The doorbell rang. Then there was pounding. Then ringing again. It was hard to ignore that.

Evan opened the door and several men wearing

fishing hats piled into the room bringing the odor of lake water and expensive scotch with them.

"Tess!" And there was Henry, grinning at her.

She managed a smile. "Hi, Henry."

"You sang to my employees, Tess."

"Sorry about that."

"Oh, no! I hear they loved it. Went right back to work all refreshed."

Tess laughed. She couldn't help it.

"Hear you've been canoodling with my great-nephew, too."

"Serious canoodling," Evan said.

"Serious enough that you aren't answering your phone." Henry gave him a look.

"Well…" Evan began.

"Say no more," Henry said.

"Is anyone hungry? I've got sandwiches." Anything for a distraction, Tess thought. "They're leftovers, but they're still good."

There was general agreement so Tess went to get the plate of sandwiches out of the fridge, following the conversation from the kitchen.

"Thanks for what you did," Henry said to Evan. "Everything is fine now."

"But Alliance—"

"*That* was a mistake," said one of the other men as Tess brought in the sandwiches. "I've rescinded all stock purchase offers and I've sold Henry the stock Alliance purchased during our vacation. Everything is as it was when he left."

Henry sat on the arm of the sofa and took a sandwich. "That's Jeffrey Sargent, Alliance's CEO. We've also got Colton's CEO and a couple of others here. We're all fishing buddies."

Evan looked aghast. "But…but they're our competitors."

"Which is why we all go fishin' together at the same time. Keep our eye on each other. Nobody makes a move during fishing."

"And I am embarrassed to have caused you so much trouble," Jeffrey apologized. "Clearly, I didn't word the memo to my executive director strongly enough."

"Don't worry about it," Henry waved off the apology. "You've got yourself a real go-getter there. A takeover made perfect business sense to him."

But Jeffrey shook his head. "The one thing that keeps me going is knowing I can take two weeks off every year and not have to worry about you yahoos going after me."

"Hear, hear!" said the others.

"'Keep your friends close and your enemies closer,'" Evan quoted.

Henry gave a great guffaw. "Exactly."

They ate the sandwiches and decided that they'd go back to the lake for another couple of days—though they refused to say exactly where this lake was located.

After the other men had left, Henry followed Tess and Evan into the kitchen. "I saw the suitcase and a duffel bag that still looks mighty heavy. Are you coming or going, Tess?"

She looked at Evan, rather than Henry. "Going."

"Not without me, you're not." Evan calmly opened the dishwasher and added the sandwich plate.

Did they have to have this conversation in front of Henry? "Henry, I'm not taking Evan away from you. And I wish I could stay and join Bartholomew's Best—"

"Don't believe you've been asked."

Inexplicably miffed, she said, "Well, I'm certainly qualified!"

"I know."

"Except for the panic attacks," she added.

"Evan mentioned those when he quit just now."

"Quit what?"

"My job." Evan rinsed the glasses.

She stared at his back. "When were you planning on telling me?"

"Haven't had a chance." He sent a look over his shoulder at his uncle.

He'd quit. For her. Foolish man. "You can't quit a family."

"I did."

"I can't let you."

"Too late."

"Oh, such drama. To be young again. Or maybe not." Henry sat at the kitchen table. "You don't want to leave Evan, Tess. You love him."

Tess threw her arms in the air. "*Everyone* knows."

"Yes."

"I love her, too," Evan told Henry.

"Of course you do."

"Henry—Evan. Henry," she said firmly. "I need to

return your money. Or most of it. I spent some on rent and a lot on underwear." She couldn't believe she said that.

Henry gave a crack of laughter.

Evan sent her a long look, then wiped his hands and came over to her. "If you leave, I leave. If you stay, I stay." He took her hands. "You're not just the most important thing in my life, you *are* my life."

"But Evan…what will you do?"

He raised his eyebrows. "You want me to tell you with Henry sitting there?"

Incredibly, she felt her cheeks warm. "I mean—jobwise."

"We travel and we take each day as it comes. You tried my kind of life and it doesn't work for you. So now, I'll try yours." He folded her in his arms.

It felt so good to be in his arms. Tess exhaled a shaky breath. Oh, it sounded perfect, but how could she drag him around with her? But how could she leave him?

"Very touching," said Henry.

"Henry, go away. Tess and I want to be alone."

"But I have an idea."

They looked at him.

"Field researchers. You two take to the road and travel around looking for products for the store. Send me a report every month or six weeks or if that's too much pressure, every quarter."

"You mean, get out there and mingle with people?" Evan asked. "Research? And maybe look for locations for possible expansion?"

Henry shrugged. "I'm open."

"Where would we go?" Tess asked.

"Anywhere," Henry said.

"So, you'd give us jobs to travel around and see what we see?" she asked him, just to make certain.

"And report, yes."

"And evaluate products?" Evan asked. "Maybe add new ones?"

Henry nodded.

Evan gazed sternly at him. "And you'd pay attention to what we say?"

"Sure."

Tess knew where Evan was going with this. "Even if it wasn't what you wanted to hear?"

Henry frowned. "I don't have to like it, do I?"

They shook their heads.

"I suppose," Henry conceded grudgingly. "So you'll consider it?"

Henry might have tossed off his plan as though it had just come to him, but Tess saw the seriousness in his eyes and she responded to it the way she'd responded to the wisdom that had made him her favorite customer over the past year.

Tess gazed up at Evan, feeling hope for the first time. "Hey, it works for me. Except, I know you had plans for the store. You sure?"

"Plans change when something better comes along. And you're something better."

Tess looked into his eyes and saw patience and love. She drew a breath, a calm, lung-filling breath, and said, "Let's do it."

"I think you should seal the deal with a kiss, Evan."

"I think you should leave, Henry, because I intend to seal it with a lot more than that."

"Isn't it beautiful?" Tess asked days later.

She and Evan were giving tours of their new, luxury RV, their home on wheels, that Tess had bought with Henry's money.

It was the end of June and a crowd of Bartholomews had come to see them off.

Quatro sat in the driver's seat. "What kind of gas mileage does this thing get?"

"Don't ask," Evan said.

"I can't believe all the stuff that's in here," Jos said. "It's like a really, really, really efficient apartment. Except the bed is huge."

"Custom order." Tess poked Evan with her elbow.

He encircled her waist from the back. "The computer station is custom, as well. But I won't be spending nearly as much time there."

"I can't believe there's a spa bathtub as well as a shower in here." Evan's parents had returned and his mother was admiring the bathroom. "And the decor—there's nothing stodgy about it. This place looks like a chic New York apartment."

"Thanks," Tess said. "My mom's work."

Yes, she'd called her mother and made nice. It was easier to forgive when she was happy, not that her clueless mother realized she'd needed to be forgiven, but, well, she'd been great with the design help for the RV. Maybe it was just a matter of knowing how to talk to her.

Evan's mother took her hand and Evan's. "Now, listen. I've resigned myself to the fact that you two are going to elope—"

"Mom," Evan said in warning.

"Pish. Everyone can see that you two are besotted with each other."

Tess just shook her head.

"But if you get an inkling that it's about to happen and there's time, just give us a quick call and I'll fly to wherever you two are immediately. I'll charter a plane. Anything."

"Barbara!" Evan's father spoke up. "Do you know what it costs to charter a plane?"

"I'm sure you'll tell me." Evan's mother squeezed and released their hands. "Call!"

"Don't let her pressure you," Evan said after his parents and the others had left.

Tess thought a moment, testing the idea. It wasn't as though it should be a surprise to her. Evan was all about family. "You know, I'm glad she brought it up. Maybe it'll give you the right idea."

He drew her to him. "I've always had the right idea about you."

"Hmm. That's a little vague. I was hoping for more of a commitment here."

"You want a commitment? You?"

"Yes. We're going to be traveling all around, meeting new people—I want all those hot women out there to know you're off the market."

He rested his forehead against hers. "I am so off the market."

"Good. Me, too."

"I never thought I'd hear you say that. Never."

She leaned up to kiss him. "And that's why you should never say never."

EVAN MANEUVERED the RV away from the liquor store. "Tess, if we're going to a party in a bar, why do we have to bring our own stuff to drink?"

"When Cat called, she told me that there'd been a fire. A huge blaze destroyed the warehouse where the supplies were kept, so it's BYOB."

"Temptation just can't get a break."

"Well, it looks like everybody has ended up okay. I mean, Laine is married!"

"You could be married," Evan said. "Say the word."

"Let's wait until we find the perfect place."

"Not the word," Evan grumbled good-naturedly.

"I'm eager for you to meet everyone. You didn't really get a chance that day." And Tess was looking forward to seeing her friends again, too.

They'd be surprised at all the changes in her life and from what she'd heard, they had their own changes.

It was funny, she thought, reaching over and rubbing Evan's shoulder, that so much good could come out of the bar closing. That day, they'd acted as if the world had ended and it was true that way of life had. But that wasn't necessarily a bad thing.

"After the party, where do you want to go?" Evan asked. "North, south, east, or west?"

Tess gave him a misty smile. "I'm already right where I want to be."

The
Temptation
Years
1984–2005

<u>Autographs</u>

Temptation~
Thanks for the memories
Barbara Daly

Temptation is and always
will be home. The line
and its readers gave me
my start. I love you all!
Carly Phillips

Temptation always had the heroines I
wanted to be - and the heroes I wanted
to have!

Cindi Myers

Thanks for the memories,
Temptation! And thanks
especially for putting me
in touch with so many
wonderful readers. I'll miss you.
Cara Summers

I ♡ Temptations!
I made my Harlequin
debut there & found
some of my 'fave
authors between
Temptation covers.
Temptresses RULE!
Dawn Atkins

I'll miss our steamy
nights and laughs, chica!
Julie McBride

My dear Temptation.

What can I say? You've given me some wonderful reads, launched my career, and introduced me to a whole slew of new friends. You had a fabulous run and I'll miss you!

Love,
Julie Kenner

Dear Temptation,
Thanks for giving this
naive girl a chance to be
"just a little bit naughty."
Dorien Kelly K.

It is with great sadness I say goodbye to Temptation. So many wonderful stories... So many great authors. Thanks to editors Brenda Chin and Jennifer Green for giving me a home, and to the Temptesses for making me feel so welcome!

All my best,

Jill Monroe

Dear Temptation,

You were the first Harlequin line I fell in love with as a reader, and the line I felt honored to break into as an author.

Colleen Collins

Thanks for my ten tempting years!
Heather MacAllister
June 1995 - June 2005

For all the friends I've made
and stories I've loved -- It was
my pleasure to be led into Temptation
Suzanne D'Alessandro

Thanks for giving me my
start! I'll always be
a "Temptation" writer.
Kate Hoffmann

Dear Temptation--

What a run! As a reader,
I learned anything is
possible if you approach
life with a little sass.

Heck, I learned the same
as a writer.
Here's to sass!
*Jennifer Elizabeth
Loto*

"Temptation" was right there at the
start of SEXY and HOT. She'll be
remembered with love and a
quickened pulse by
Barbara Delinsky

My love and undying gratitude
to my readers. I couldn't have
enjoyed seventeen fabulous years
at Temptation without you!
Kristine Rolofson

Temptation will always
have a home on my bookshelf!
KRISTIN GABRIEL

First Kiss. First love. First book.
I'll never forget the Temptation!
Smooches,
Cherry

My keeper shelf is stuffed
full of Temptation stories
and I've loved every month
of this awesome line! Thanks
for all the great reading :)
Joanne Rock

Writing for the Temptation line
helped me to find my voice as
a writer. I'm proud to be
forever linked to this line as
a Temptress! Stephanie Bond

Happy retirement,
Temptation!
You've brought me so
much joy and laughter
through the years. It's
hard to watch you go.
— Wendy Etherington

For years, Temptations were the books I loved to read. Becoming a Temptress was a dream come true and forged lasting friendships with both authors and readers. Thank you, Temptation, for the fun, laughter, and good times!

Janelle Denison

Not only did Temptation give me my start, it also gave me some of the greatest friends of my life. I'll always be honored to have been a Temptress!
Leslie Kelly

Thanks to Harlequin — You let your writers spread their wings and fly. We're touched the sky.
Sandra Chastain

Thank you, Temptation, for giving me special friends I'll value for a lifetime. The camaraderie and talent within the line, and the readers who gave it popularity, made writing for Temptation a very special time in my life. I'll miss the fun more than I can say.
Lori Foster

My very first book was a
Temptation, so the line will
always hold a special place in
my heart.

I wish all the talented
authors, brilliant editors and, most
of all, the faithful readers all the
best for the future.

Always a Temptress!
Nancy Warren

From getting that first call
for CALL ME on national televisio
to being a part of the line's
15th Anniversary... thanks,
Temptation, for all of the
memories! Alison Kent

There's nothing like diving into a chat, totally
fun story — I have only the best memories
of writing for Temptation.
Carla Neggers

Temptation Romances taught me to believe. Not only
in the power of love, but also in the power of
being a woman. Being published in the line
was the ultimate expression of all the things
I learned from the line, independence, belief in
myself, and faith that success on every level was
within my grasp. Thank you HQ for giving women
strong, sexy role models to show them the way!

Marie Fox

Hey, sweet Temptation! What a kick hanging out with you. Thanks for the memories! XX OO Vicki Lewis Thompson

True love stories never have endings — Friends 4-ever! Lori & Tony aka Tori Carrington

Jolaine Rose

I can resist everything but Temptations!! Kathleen O'Reilly

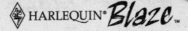